BROKEN PANE

BROKEN PANE

A LONESOME, PARTY OF SIX COMPANION NOVEL

A. AINSWORTH

1

"Hey, Boss, I've got some bad news. I've been over here mowing leaves at Winding Acres. I was almost finished when I ran over a rock and slung it into a resident's window. Bad timing, I know, day before Thanksgiving and all. I'm sorry for inconveniencing you before the holiday."

"Okay, slow down, Hunt. Tell me what you have done about it so far."

"I told the lady at the front desk, and I duct taped some heavy cardboard inside and out of the window. There's no danger of any of the residents cutting themselves. Boss, I'm really sorry about this. I realize the timing stinks."

"Don't worry about it. Not the first time we've broken a window. Did you make sure you didn't leave any glass on the floor or the window ledge?"

"The window just spider webbed, so there's not any glass lying around anywhere. I figured I'd tape it up just to be on the safe side, though. Being this close to Thanksgiving, I didn't know how quick we'd be able to get somebody out to the retirement home to take care of it."

"No, you did good, Hunt. Before you head to your next job, send me a picture of the window and send me some measurements. I'll call the glass place and talk to my buddy who has replaced a couple of other windows for me. I'm sure he wouldn't be able to get to it until after the weekend, but I'll get something lined up. Thanks for calling me right away."

"Uh, boss, one more thing. This may or may not be important for your glass guy."

"What is it, Hunt?"

"The lady at the desk seemed a little disturbed when we walked outside, and she saw which window I broke, even though I assured her we would replace it, and they didn't have to worry about a thing. When we walked back inside to her desk, she called one of the cleaning crew to the front desk and asked if Mr. Perdue was in his room. She said no, that he was in the library working on his book. The lady at the desk told the cleaning lady to show me to his room so I could tape up the inside of his window. I explained to her that only the outside pane was broken, but she asked me to tape in up, anyway. I didn't want to argue with her since I had already broken the window, so I just did what she asked, but I wanted you to know why I covered up the inside, too.

"While we were walking down the hall toward his room, the cleaning lady muttered, 'Of all the rooms in this place...' I don't understand what she meant by that, but both the cleaning lady and the lady at the front desk asked me how soon I thought we could get the window replaced. They seemed to be real anxious, more than you might expect, you know?"

"Hmm, I don't know, but you send me those measurements, and I'll get started on replacing it. If Greg can't get to it, I'll go down there in the morning and install the new one."

"You install glass, boss?"

"If it's tinted double-paned tempered glass like I think it is, all it'll take is a razor knife, rubber stripping, and caulk. I have watched Greg do it enough times that I'm pretty sure I can do it myself. If not, I'm sure I can find an instructional video online. You can learn a lot that way, Hunt."

"Sure can. So, after I send you photos and measure-ments, I'm good to move on to the next job? It's my last one of the day. I was hoping to be halfway through it by now."

"Yeah, that's all I need. I'll see you back at the shop later this afternoon."

"TRIPLE G GLASS, may I help you?" Greg Smith was the second of the G's in the company name. His father, Glen, has started the company in the '70s, and Greg and his younger brother Gary had taken over when Glen retired two years earlier. Greg led a men's Bible study at the church David had attended since high school. They had prayed for him during his Army stint and even sent him a care package when he was stuck in Iraq for Christmas.

"Hey, Greg, this is David Gull."

"David Gull, what can I do for you on the afternoon before Thanksgiving, my young friend?"

"Bad timing, I know. One of my guys slung a rock into a window at a retirement home this afternoon, and they're pretty anxious about getting it replaced as soon as possible. I don't guess by some chance you're going to be over near Winding Acres in Harriston this afternoon, are you?"

"No, I sent a guy out that way this morning for a mirror install before we finished up our bigger jobs, but both of my crews are back cleaning up the shop and getting ready for a long weekend. We could get over there Tuesday or Wednesday of next week."

"Any chance I could pick up a window from you this afternoon and put it in myself? Normally, I would have you do the job, but like I said, they want it done sooner than I figured you'd be able to get to it. I don't understand what they're so nervous about, but the broken pane was our fault, so I want to make it right and get it done by tomorrow if I can. I've seen you do it often enough that I believe I can do it if you'll make sure I've got what I need."

"Yeah, man, we can make that happen. What size are you looking at installing?"

"Thirty-six wide by fifty-four tall, tinted, double pane, tempered glass, black frame."

Greg laughed. "Wow, you sound like a glass man,

David. You're not thinking about starting up another business to compete with me, are you? I can't have you stealing my customers by working cheap and working on holidays and all."

"No way. I've just hung out with you enough to be able to talk the lingo. Working with glass scares me, but this one is framed, so I should be good, right?"

Yeah, and that's a pretty standard size, too, so... hold on, I'm looking... yeah, we've got several that size. Any chance you can you get over here by 4:00? We were hoping to leave early today, but I can wait on you a little while if you need."

"No need for that. Let me make a quick phone call, and I'll head that way. Give me twenty minutes."

On the way to the glass shop, David called Winding Acres to apologize again for the broken window. He promised to be there to replace it at 8:00 when they unlocked the front doors. The receptionist thanked him profusely. What was it about this Mr. Perdue that had all the Winding Acres employees on edge, he wondered. He supposed he would find out on Thanksgiving morning. With no plans until late afternoon, he didn't mind the unexpected opportunity to model the customer service he expected of himself and his team.

TWO HOURS LATER, David returned to his shop with everything he needed for the repair. Hunt had told the other guys of his ill-timed incident and why the boss was running a little late. David walked into a tidy shop full of clean and serviced equipment, ready for work Monday morning.

"Hunt," he bellowed from the door at the front of the shop. "Come give me a hand, would you?"

"Ooooh," the others teased.

Moments later, David and Hunt returned to the shop with two large coolers full of turkeys for David's employees. After distributing the frozen birds, thanking his guys for their work as he did every day, and wishing them a happy Thanksgiving, he locked the shop for the holiday weekend. Everything but Mr. Perdue's window would wait until Monday.

2

R azor knife, hand broom, and dustpan in hand, David was standing at the front door of the Winding Acres Retirement Community at 7:55. Winding Acres was the first commercial account for his mowing business after nine years of residential work. From his start cutting yards for senior citizens on his street as a twelve-year-old, his neighborhood business had grown steadily until he earned his driver's license and expanded into other areas of Harriston, Mississippi, a college town of fifty thousand. Once he added a truck and trailer to his arsenal, he added enough business that he needed additional manpower. Hunt was one of his first hires and one who had helped maintain the business while David did a three-year tour in the Army.

Guys like Hunt were essential to the thriving business. They treated customers like the business was theirs. It was, in a way. When David incorporated the business after his return from his last tour in Iraq, he named it Gull & Associates, though he was the sole proprietor. He instituted a profit-sharing plan to incentivize his now twelve-person team to give their customers the best service in the lawn care business and to treat them like they wanted to be treated. He had used last year's slower winter months to train his team in everything from customer service to sales to several new services they would offer in the spring.

One of David's points of emphasis was adding commercial accounts to the residential side of his business. The four guys who kept the business going during his three-year absence knew the values of the company almost as well as he did. After a little sales training, he sent them out to twenty hand-picked properties to sell them on the benefits of doing business with Gull & Associates. Whit Orland landed the Winding Acres account during the first week of sales calls and added two more the following week. David rewarded Whit by making him his first account manager after the sales team brought in two more commercial accounts. Business was booming, and David was twenty-two years old.

No matter how much success his company enjoyed, David valued having a troubleshooter available to take care of unexpected needs like this broken window. He always assigned the responsibility to one of his employees or took it himself. Whit enjoyed the role since it gave him a chance to get out of the office on occasion, but since he was out of town visiting his wife's family, the task fell to David. When the front door to Winding Acres swung open at 8:00, he stepped inside right on time, as he had promised.

———

LESS THAN FIVE YEARS OLD, Winding Acres was still the newest retirement facility in town. The grounds were immaculate when the place opened, but David noticed when he returned to town from Iraq that the grounds crew that won the original contract had taken shortcuts. He had watched the crew from You Grow It, We Mow It Lawn Service trim the border of the flowerbeds to the dirt one week, then skip the string trimming altogether the following week. This saved time and made You Grow It more money, but it didn't seem to match the standards of Winding Acres. When Whit had pointed out the shortcuts in his sales call to the manager, he assured him Gull & Associates would take care of the grounds as if their job depended on it.

"David?"

"Yes, ma'am, David Gull."

"You're the owner of Gull & Associates?"

"Yes, ma'am, I am. How are you this morning?"

"I'm fine. How old are you?"

He was used to the question in its various degrees of brusqueness. "I'm twenty-two. Started this business with one yard when I was twelve." That line put the customers at ease when they questioned his experience. Now that he was officially ten years in, he could add,

"We've been providing our clients the best lawn care in the business for the last ten years." *Clients* had a better ring to it than *customers*, he had learned. Language mattered. He informed the graying receptionist that he was here for his *8:00 appointment* to *install* a *new window* in place of the one that *his company broke*. Every word was genuine, not salesy, but he had learned that using responsible, respectful language was key to winning customer loyalty as long as his company lived up to their words. And it did.

His approach served its purpose. The receptionist introduced herself as Jeanette Powers and escorted him to Room 1108 in the east wing of the building. "This is Mr. Perdue's room. He's in the dining area right now, and he'll be in the library working on his book the rest of the morning, at least until you're finished. At least that's what he told me yesterday afternoon when I broke the news about his window. He didn't seem as upset about it as I expected, so I guess that's good."

"Is he an avid reader?"

"Mr. Perdue? Yes, I suppose, but he'll be busy *writing* his book. At least that's what he claims. He's been working on it since he arrived here almost a year ago. It's his first book. He says he's telling the story of how he ended up here, but he won't tell us much about it. He tells us we'll have to buy the book to find out."

"That's cool. One of my mom's friends wrote her story and published it this year. She and her husband adopted two African-American twin boys and during the process, she found out she was pregnant with twin girls."

"Oh, my word. Is either set of twins identical?"

"Both. Tall, athletic black sons and beautiful blonde daughters. It's a cool book, easy to read. The twins are all in their mid-twenties now and married, but there are some fascinating stories about their adventures growing up. If you like to read, you should pick up a copy. I could get you a signed one if you'd like."

"What's the book called? I might want to read that if I can remember the title."

"Oh, you'll be able to remember it, all right. She called it *Two of a Kind: Working on an Empty House*. Carol Turner is her name."

DAVID STEPPED INSIDE and saw that Hunt's window cover had been peeled away and was lying on the floor to the right of the window. He could see the outside broken pane through the unbroken inner pane. Everything seemed to be pretty standard. "All right, Ms. Jeanette, let's hope this is as simple a task as it appears. Let me run out to my truck to fetch my tools, and I should have Mr. Perdue fixed up before his Thanksgiving lunch."

"That would be great. He can be an odd bird sometimes. You can see the cardboard your guy put over the window sitting on the floor. He didn't seem too upset about the window when I told him about it yesterday afternoon, but he came back to the desk later all in a tizzy about the cardboard. He made me promise we would never cover up his window again."

"Yes, ma'am. He wasn't in any danger of getting cut since the inside pane wasn't broken, but my guy was just using an abundance of caution. I'm sorry for any inconvenience our accident has caused Mr. Perdue."

"Oh, he's harmless, just a little quirky. To be honest, he is younger and more energetic than our typical resident. He seems to think it's a game when any of the staff attempt to get to know him, and he shuts us out. When and if he ever publishes his book—if there really is one —I guess we'll find out why."

"Yes, ma'am. I'll be right back."

"You a coffee drinker, young man?"

"Yes, ma'am—three years in the Army and all. I'm not an alcohol drinker, so I learned to appreciate a good cup of joe."

"Stop off in the dining hall and pour yourself a cup of our gourmet blend before you start on Mr. Perdue's window. I hate you had to come out on Thanksgiving morning. It really could've waited until next week. You might as well enjoy some coffee while you work."

"I appreciate it, and I'll stop by to pour a cup on my way to Mr. Perdue's room, but replacing his window is not a problem for me. I'm not married yet, so I had some free time before my sister and her husband have everybody over to their house to eat late this afternoon. Thank you for the offer, though. I didn't leave myself enough time to stop by the coffee shop and get a cup this morning. It's probably not even open on Thanksgiving, anyway."

As David was walking by the dining hall on his way to his truck, he noticed a man sitting alone at a table just inside the door, staring at him as he walked past. He struck David as too young to be living here. He didn't dress in khakis and royal blue button-downs like other Winding Acres staff, so he must be a resident. David guessed early sixties. The gentleman dressed in stylish jeans, a short-sleeved dark green polo, and polished loafers with bright orange printed socks, though David could not discern the design.

His toolbag in one hand and insulated coffee cup in the other, David returned to the building moments later. He turned into the dining hall, scanning the room for the coffeepot. The man David had noticed earlier piped up, "Looking for the coffee dispenser, young fella?"

"Yes, sir," David answered, turning to face him.

"Far corner up there."

"Thanks. Mind if I sit my tools down here next to your table while I pour my coffee?"

"Help yourself."

David perked up a little, just smelling the coffee as he poured. *No wonder this place is so expensive. They don't cut corners, even on the coffee.* When he returned to his bag, its guardian asked, "You here to replace my window?"

"Are you Mr. Perdue?"

"The one and only."

"Then, yes, sir, I'm here to take care of your window. I'm sorry we broke it."

"*We*? Did it take more than one of you?"

David laughed nervously. "No, sir, just one, but the way I look at it, if one of us breaks a window, we all break it. That said, the guy who was working here sends along his apologies for your inconvenience, too. "

"And you drew the short straw to come out on Thanksgiving to replace a pane that could have stayed broken until next week? What does a lawn maintenance man know about replacing a window, anyway?"

David chuckled. "Well, I'm actually the owner of the company. We take great pride in our work, so when we have an accident like yesterday, we try to make it right as quickly as possible, even if it happens on the day before Thanksgiving. So here I am."

"What gives with your man mowing on the day before Thanksgiving, anyway? The grass hasn't been growing for weeks. Y'all aren't that far behind, are you?"

David liked Perdue's pointed humor. It reminded him of his sergeant's during some of his outfit's less tense times while serving in Iraq. "We use our mowers to help with leaf cleanup, too. It's a lot more efficient than a bunch of rakes and bags."

"I guess so. You still didn't say what qualifies a yard man to be a window repairman."

"Unfortunately, this is not our first broken window. I have helped the glass guy before, and yours is a pretty simple installation."

"Says you. You make a practice of going around breaking your customers' windows, do you?"

"No, sir, but with ten years in the business, it has happened a few times."

"Son, you're too young to have been doing this for ten years."

"Well, if you don't mind my saying so, you're too young to be living in a retirement home."

"Touché. Have a seat, son. My window will wait."

"Yes, sir." *Whew, thought I had spoken out of turn there for a minute.* David pulled out a chair and sat. "Turkeys on your socks. Well played, Mr. Perdue."

"So how old are you, kid?"

"Just turned twenty-two. You?"

"I'm sixty-eight, even though I don't look a day over sixty." The older man chuckled, but he spoke truth. "Help me understand the math of a twenty-two-year-old owning his own company and claiming ten years' experience."

"Started with one yard on my street when I was twelve. Built up my clientele in the neighborhood until I could drive. Hired good people who kept it going while I did time in the Army and started doing commercial properties in the last few months. How does a healthy man who doesn't even look sixty end up living at Winding Acres?"

"Only child of older parents. Mother died in childbirth. Father committed suicide two weeks later. Ward of the state until I went to college. Lived in a tree for a while. Self-made millionaire living here for that good coffee."

"O-kay."

"Every word of that is true, Mr...."

"David Gull." David extended his hand.

Feeling the firmness of his new acquaintance's handshake, the mysterious man said, "Herschel Perdue. Just call me *Perdue*. No *mister* required. Nice to meet you, Mr. Gull. That's a solid handshake you've got there."

"Thanks. Nice to meet you, too. So, your story sounds fascinating. Is that why you're writing a book?"

Perdue motioned David closer. "Did Jeanette send you to pry some information from me?"

"No," David whispered back, "but she seemed awful curious about your story. I don't make a habit of sharing information that's not mine to share, so whatever you decide to tell me stays right here."

Perdue drew even closer. "They can't stand it that I won't share anything with them. They realize there's bound to be more to me than an old chap put out to pasture by his family. I give them the eccentric old-timer routine so they'll leave me alone, but they feel like they have to know everything about the residents. I guess that's beneficial in some ways, but I just tell them if they want to know my story, they'll have to buy the book. In the meantime, I enjoy keeping them in the dark. They have no idea whether I'm even writing a book, and I think it's funny to keep them all guessing. If nobody else reads my story, I figure they will."

"I'll read it, too." Leaning back in his chair, David took a sip of his coffee. "Mm, this is fine coffee. I see why you live here."

Perdue laughed. "I like you, kid. What inspired you to mow yards at twelve years old?"

David related his mom's struggles as a single mom, his sister's passion for the books, and his pull toward hard work, ROTC, and the US Army.

"Military family?"

"Not really. My great-grandfather served in World War II, but other than that, none that I know of."

"What was your draw to the service?"

"I liked the order and discipline, and I figured I needed that in my life. Sports wasn't really my thing, so I turned to ROTC. Plus, Mom took good care of my sister and me, but there was no way she was going to afford to send us to college. My sister was super smart and involved in student government in high school, so she had more than enough in scholarships to go to college. She graduated with a degree in accounting last year. I figured I could join the Army, serve my country, and then go to college when I came home. I'm taking two night classes a semester and an online class that I work on during my lunch break. It'll take me a while to get my degree with the business hopping like it is now, but so far, I'm managing."

"Your dad in the picture at all?"

"Met him for the first time the weekend after Thanksgiving last year. Mom tracked him down in Texas a month earlier and drove out to make some things right from over twenty years earlier. Dad left before my sister turned two and while Mom was still pregnant with me. Long story short, God changed both of them a great deal last year, so they made amends. Lisa—that's my sister—and I decided we wanted to meet him, so he came to Harriston for a long weekend. One thing led to another, and he and Mom remarried weeks after I met him for the first time. They were technically still married, but they wanted to start fresh. I don't know if you believe in God, Mr. Perdue, but He has done an amazing work in my mom and dad's relationship—unbelievable, really. Enough about me, though. Tell me some of your story."

"Well, I reckon you've earned that much, Mr. David Gull, spending some time with an eccentric old man on Thanksgiving morning."

3

Larry Perdue wasn't enjoying the best day of his life, not by a long shot. This was supposed to be the day he celebrated his fiftieth birthday. He wasn't expecting much, just his favorite meal of fried chicken, mashed potatoes, potato salad, and biscuits. And, of course, strawberry cake. Helen had fixed him the same supper for twenty years now. She hadn't inquired if he wanted anything different for the last ten. Not that he minded the routine. It was the story of his last twenty years.

Maybe the guys at the plant would remember his birthday and put together a surprise party, even though they didn't make a habit of doing those types of things. Perhaps somebody would remember—after all, he had dropped a few hints over the previous months. Nothing doing, though, he discovered as soon as he entered the break room to stash his leftovers in the top back left corner of the refrigerator, where he hoped it would be left alone. Today was Bobby Waldrop Day at the plant. At twenty-one years old, Bobby became a father last night and showed up first thing this morning to pass out cigars. He was all anybody could talk about for the eight working hours of Larry's fiftieth birthday.

At least Helen would remember. She always did, even if her gifts were of the practical variety—a rake, a car waxing kit, a transistor radio so he could listen to the Cardinals on KMOX. She was an old soul, probably his fault. He was thirty when they married, ancient by the day's standard. She was twenty, a baby by comparison, but she was a good wife. She took care of their home during World War II while he led every type of drive in town, from the scrap metal drives to the paper drives to the rubber drives. Even at his age, Larry wanted to be in Europe fighting the Nazis or in the Pacific fighting the Japanese, but the Great Depression had taken its toll on his teeth. His life entailed one story after another of not measuring up to the standard.

After the war came the Baby Boom. It seemed their little Detroit neighborhood doubled in size in just the few years after the war. For Larry and Helen, it was an exercise in putting on cheerful faces as the neighbors added one, two, three, four, even five children to their families in the years following the war. One day, they looked up to find themselves the only childless couple on the street.

It wasn't as if they didn't want children. Larry had stopped bringing it up. He knew Helen wanted a baby worse than anything, and he blamed himself for not being able to give her one. They were content enough with the lives they had built for themselves, but the elephant in the room wiggled between them when either of them tried to move closer to the other. Their talks no longer involved their hopes and dreams, just their cares of the day. It wasn't a terrible life, Larry tried once again to convince himself. He looked forward to the strawberry cake and wondered what tool Helen might add to his collection this year.

Turning onto Edison Avenue, Larry counted the children under ten as he passed yard after yard of kids playing on front lawns. Except for rainy days, that number surpassed twenty on most days as he covered the two blocks to the Perdue house. He counted thirty-one on this, his fiftieth birthday. Some children had been born to children like Bobby Waldrop at work. He reminded God of the inherent unfairness of young men fresh enough to be his children, having sons and daughters of their own. *Can You not spare one child, God?* Immediately, Larry regretted the thought. *Of course He had a Son, one He didn't spare. I'm sorry, Lord.*

Still battling his inner turmoil, Larry turned his '51 Buick Roadmaster Riviera into his driveway. He had bought the car brand new, but it was only a temporary fix for his loneliness, three thousand dollars for a bandaid. Before he pulled under the carport, he mentally hung his anxieties on the lamppost in the yard. The childlessness wasn't Helen's fault, and any angst he brought home after counting the children in the neighborhood on his drive home had proved counterproductive. It wasn't worth dampening Helen's spirt, not today of all days. He killed the engine, rolled up his window, and counted to twenty before reaching for the handle.

Larry was stepping from the Buick when he remembered his birthday again. It occurred to him for the first time that Helen might struggle with this birthday. After all, he was fifty, and she was thirty-nine. She would be forty in fifteen days, but their ages might as well have been twenty years apart for what it sounded like. He knew she wasn't looking forward to turning forty, but he hadn't considered what his turning fifty would do to her. The big round number didn't bother him much— that is until Bobby Waldrop showed up with cigars to steal his thunder. It probably didn't matter since nobody even mentioned his birthday, but why couldn't Bobby have shown up tomorrow? Because tomorrow was Saturday, of course. *Stop it! Hang that stuff on the lamppost and go inside.*

Helen hadn't forgotten. Good ol' Helen. He could see her through the screen door to the kitchen, standing over the stove, her petite figure still resembling a younger woman's. The aroma of fried chicken wafted through the screen, an invitation to celebrate. How many nights had she cooked for two, hoping she would one day cook for three or four or more? He was working at a service station in his mid-twenties when he first laid eyes on her. His boss had asked him to deliver the principal's '26 Packard with its new carburetor. She was eating lunch with her friends under one of the shade trees in front of the school when he pulled up in front of the office. Her beautiful blond hair captured his attention, and she noticed him because he was driving Mr. Adamson's car.

Though the glance they exchanged only lasted a couple of seconds before her bashfulness forced her eyes away, Larry and Helen crossed paths again two years later. She had graduated and was working in her father's furniture store when Larry walked in one day to buy a couch for his new house. He introduced himself as though the glance in the schoolyard never happened, and she answered his furniture questions like she would have for any other customer. However, the interest was still intact, still mutual. She tested him by saying how unusual it was that he was there to pick out the couch instead of his wife. He savored the opportunity to tell her he lived alone in a brand new house and that he was still waiting on the right woman before he tied the knot. After a few dates, she relished the opportunity to become that woman, and they married six months later.

Her father had not been too happy about the age gap at first, but her mother gently reminded him of their own eight-year difference. They warmed up to Larry, found him to be a responsible man who would treat their daughter right and be a good father to their grandchildren. They were half right. Larry and Helen were both devastated when her parents died in a house fire ten years later, still without grandchildren. His parents were dead, too, and neither of them had any surviving brothers or sisters. The elephant that stood between them was the end of the line for both families, and there was nothing either seemed able to do about it.

"Are you coming in?" Helen shouted over the frying chicken.

"Huh, what?" Larry asked, embarrassed that his thoughts had taken him away like they did more and more these days.

"Are you planning to come in for your birthday celebration or stand there like a knot on a pickle?" So the fiftieth anniversary of his birth was a *knot on a pickle* day. Other days, she claimed he was *standing there like a bump on a log* when he spaced out, lost in the thoughts he rarely shared with her anymore.

"I'm coming, I'm coming. I was just taking a whiff of supper and admiring the beauty of the cook. You look especially gorgeous tonight, Mrs. Perdue."

"All right, Mr. Perdue, flattery will get you everywhere." After he swung the screen door wide, she met him at the threshold before he mounted the top step and kissed him while their heads were still level. "Get on in here, birthday boy. I'm fixing your favorites."

"How do you know they're still my favorites? You haven't asked in probably ten years." He hadn't intended on letting the question escape his lips, any more than he had in the previous years since she had last asked. He wished he wouldn't have. She looked crestfallen.

"Larry, I'm sorry. I just thought…" Snapping back to her bright demeanor, she asked, "For future reference, what should I cook as your one most special meal?"

"This." He reached down to kiss her on the cheek. "This is perfect. I was just messing with you."

She swatted him with the kitchen towel she was

holding in her hand. "Well, I've got a special surprise for you after supper."

"Strawberry cake?"

"Still your favorite?"

"Still my favorite."

"Well, I made a strawberry cake, but there's more."

"What is it?"

"Well, it wouldn't be a surprise after supper if I told you now, would it? Go get cleaned up. It'll be ready in twenty minutes."

"Yes, ma'am," he said, giving her rear end a tiny pop on his way by.

"Supper first, mister," she said with a wink.

He returned the wink. "Dessert later."

"If you're a good boy. Now, go get cleaned up."

Supper and his birthday cake were delicious, as always, and he told her so. Homemade ice cream was a new touch, one he would gladly include in his special meal menu from then on. After Helen cleared the table, she walked to the back of the house, where Larry heard paper rattling. She returned with not one wrapped package, but two.

"Okay, this is different," he said, rubbing his palms together in anticipation. His excitement was genuine. They had agreed on one practical gift for birthdays at the beginning of their marriage, and neither had ever swayed from it until now. He had often wondered how she would respond to a more romantic gift, but since his birthday came first, he followed her lead and stuck with practical presents.

Helen pushed the larger package across the table to him. "Open this one first."

Larry made a show of carefully, slowly unwrapping his first gift. When he deliberately tore a small corner from the front of the package, he read the brand name *Vibrosage*. He didn't recognize the brand name, so this would be more of a surprise than usual. Ripping the rest of the white wrapping, Larry broke into a grin. "An electric massager. I never expected that."

"I tried for something different this year. Do you like it?"

"I don't know. Let's find out." The couple spent the next thirty minutes swapping head, shoulder, back, and foot massages with Larry's new toy and rating each experience.

When their laughter subsided, Helen reached for the other gift and pushed it across without releasing it. "I know you don't want to miss *Dragnet* on television tonight, but how about opening this one before we turn it on? The massager was a surprise, but this one's the genuine surprise. If you want to make sure you don't miss *Dragnet*, though, you might wait on this one."

"Just the facts, ma'am. Let's have it."

She released the gift. "Go!" Helen could hardly contain her excitement as Larry shredded the paper. "Well, don't you love it?"

"A... Mr. Potato Head?"

"Yes," Helen squealed. "Don't you wish you would have had these as kids? It would have been so much fun."

"I... guess."

"You don't like it."

"It's not that. It's just..."

Helen stood and grabbed the toy, her smile all but gone. She turned and strode down the hall, yelling over her shoulder, "Fine, if you don't like it, I'll just save it for our child to enjoy." She kept walking, slamming the bedroom door behind her.

Larry replayed the conversation three times in his head, trying to figure where it had gone off the tracks. It was his fault somehow, he figured, but what a way to end the day. Why didn't he just say he liked it so they could watch *Dragnet*? Or...

He tiptoed down the hall to their bedroom and cracked the door. She was standing there, hands on hips, expecting him.

"Our... child?"

"Larry, I'm pregnant!"

4

"That was you. You were the baby."

"That was me. I found out later that my mom and dad enjoyed the next seven months more than any other time in their marriage. People I talked to who knew my father said he lived most of his life thinking he was snakebit. He and Mom enjoyed a fine life together, but nothing seemed to go as planned. He wanted to be married in his early twenties like his friends were, but it was not in the cards for him. Even though he found a beautiful wife later—my mother was a stunning young woman at twenty when my dad married her—but then they couldn't have the children they both wanted. He believed his life was one story of false hope after another—until the day Mom told him she was pregnant.

"The neighbors said between the time he found out he was going to have a child—he didn't care whether I was a boy or a girl—and when was born, Dad's faith blossomed. He had been a faithful churchgoer all those years, but now he was enjoying some blessings of the Lord that everyone else in their congregation took for granted. He and Mom started dreaming again, hoping again. David, I don't know if you realize at your age just how powerful a driving force hope is. My dad needed a shot of hope, and I was it."

"Trust me, Mr. Perdue, I understand the power of hope. What happened?"

———

"LARRY, boss man sent me to get you. Your wife's on the phone, and she needs you..." Larry's wrench hit the floor behind him, trailing his mad dash for the office phone. His boss extended the receiver as soon as he burst through the door.

"Helen?!... slow down, honey...... are you sure... how far apart... on my way."

Larry skidded to a stop four steps past the office door before spinning around. "Boss, my wife's..."

"Go!"

———

"HELEN!"

"In here," she replied from the living room couch, where her bag sat at her feet.

"Ready?" he asked, reaching for her with both hands.

"Yes, help me up. Get the bag. Go slow. I'm hurting. Contractions are six minutes apart."

"Okay, got it. Let's get you to the car." With one hand on her left elbow and the other supporting her back, Larry escorted her to the passenger side of the car. He raced to the driver's side and slid behind the wheel.

Helen mustered a smile. "Don't kill us on the way."

"I won't as long as other drivers stay out of my way."

Traffic was light in the middle of the afternoon as Larry sped through the streets of their neighborhood en route to the hospital in Detroit. Twenty minutes later, he turned into the hospital's parking lot.

"Emergency room," Helen said between gritted teeth. When Larry turned to face her, she added what she dared not say while he was driving. "Something's not right."

Larry sped toward the emergency room entrance on the east side of the complex. "What is it, Helen?"

"I don't know, just a suspicion. I hope it's just the nerves of being a first-time mom."

The car screeched to a stop in front of the emergency room entrance. A few seconds later, Larry yanked Helen's door open, all the while yelling for help. An attendant pushed a wheelchair out the door by the time he had Helen on her feet.

"What's wrong?" the attendant asked.

"My wife is in labor." Larry hoped his intensity would transfer to this young man now driving Helen's wheelchair.

"Contractions?"

"Yes, about six minutes apart when we left the house."

"They're two minutes apart now," Helen updated with an urgency she hadn't shared on the drive to the hospital. "And something's wrong."

"What's wrong?"

"She can't put her finger on it, but she thinks something is not right. This is our first child, so we hope it is a false alarm." The look on the orderly's face spoke a question he dared not ask. "We're old for a first child. She's forty. Please help her."

"She'll be going straight back. You stop at the desk and get started on the paperwork. We'll get you to the right waiting room when it's time."

———

THIRTY MINUTES PASSED after Larry spoke to the orderly, and the only progress he had made was filling out a mountain of paperwork. When he signed and dated the last blank, a nurse directed him to a sterile waiting room near the labor and delivery section of the hospital. The seats in the waiting room served as nothing but obstacles for his pacing.

A man in scrubs interrupted Larry's thoughts. "Mr. Perdue?"

"Yes, that's me." Larry covered the space between him and his wife's doctor in seconds.

"Mr. Perdue, your wife was thirty weeks pregnant, is that correct?"

"Yes, that's right. Is everything okay?"

"Here's what's been happening with your wife's delivery, Mr. Perdue: When she began to push, we discovered the baby was breech, so his behind wanted to come out first."

"He?"

"A baby boy. Like I was saying, it's not uncommon for a premature baby to have not turned headfirst yet, but it means that we had to do an emergency Cesarean section. When we went to take the baby, we found his umbilical cord wrapped around his neck."

Larry gasped. "Oh, God. Is... he...?"

"We were able to take him and get him breathing. He will need a few extra days in the hospital to make sure that everything develops as it should, especially his lungs since he is early."

"When can I see him?"

"Probably not for another day or two." The doctor continued, "Mr. Perdue... your wife... she..."

Larry's knees loosened underneath him. "Say it, doctor. What is it?"

"Perhaps you'd better sit down."

Larry sank into the chair behind him, but his eyes didn't leave the doctor's. "Please..."

"When your wife realized what we were going to do to save your son, she insisted we save him. We did that, but Mr. Perdue, your wife lost a lot of blood during the delivery. We tried our best to keep them both stabilized. Mr. Perdue, I hate to tell you this, but she didn't survive the delivery."

"Dad's friends claimed he was never the same after that, as you can imagine. He wasn't just grieving. One of his neighbors that I tracked down when I was in my mid-twenties said, 'That snake had bitten Larry one time too many times.'"

"I'm so sorry," David said. "I can't imagine how difficult that must have been for him, especially with how long they had waited."

"He blamed himself. When that doctor told him how Mom had insisted on taking care of the baby—" Herschel Perdue dabbed his eyes with the corner of his napkin and paused for a slow pull of coffee. "He interpreted that as Mom thinking that I was more important to him than she was."

"Oh, no."

"Oh, yes. He walked through the next few days in a daze. Friends of theirs from church took care of everything because Dad couldn't. He was in a daze throughout her funeral and when he brought me home a week after I was born. He did not know what to do with a baby after naming me Herschel Andrew Perdue after both of Mom's grandfathers. Three ladies from the church—grandmother types from what I've been told— took turns taking care of me at their houses at night and at Dad's house during the day when I first came home. He was just going through the motions. Those ladies couldn't even be confident he was hearing any of their instructions for him the few times they left me alone with him.

"After completely caring for me for a week, they knew it was time for Dad to wean himself off of their help. Several days before he went back to work, they told him they could care for me during the day, but he would be responsible for picking me up and caring for me at night. They planned to pick me up in the morning so he could make sure he arrived at work on time. From what I've been told, he just sat there and nodded the entire time.

"They started that night leaving me with Dad, although whichever one was there that night stayed until I fell asleep. The one that picked me up the next morning said I acted like I had taken my middle-of-the-night feeding, so that was positive. They handed off more responsibilities to my dad over the next three days, like having him deliver me to the babysitter's house in the morning, and he did everything he was supposed to do. He delivered me to the sitter on time every morning and showed up at the appointed time to pick me up in the afternoon, thirty minutes after when he would leave work the following week.

"On the Sunday afternoon before he was set to return to work, he asked a lady who had been watching me to sit with me at our house one more time. He said he wanted to visit Mom's grave for an hour. It was the first time since her funeral he had wanted to talk about her, so this lady took it as a good sign and walked over to Dad's house to sit with me. When he didn't come home on time, she became worried. When he still wasn't home an hour later, she called one of the other ladies, who called some men from the church to look for him. They found him lying on Mom's grave—cold—an empty bottle of sleeping tablets still in his hands."

David buried his face in his palms. His eyes were swollen when he pulled his hands back. "Mr. Perdue, I'm at a loss for what to say. I am so sorry that you have had to carry that with you your whole life."

Perdue reached into the computer bag at his feet and produced a single sheet of paper folded like a letter. "Here is a copy of the note he left on my mother's grave. You can read it if you want, young fella." David reached for it.

Dear Son,

Before I tell you why I've done what I've done, I want you to know that none of this is your fault. Your mother and I wanted you more than anything. At our age, we assumed we would never have children, but then you came along. I found out about you on my fiftieth birthday, and there is not a better present anybody could have given me.

On the day you were born, I rushed home from work to take your mother to the hospital. You were trying to enter this world early, and we weren't quite ready for you yet, but you had other ideas. After you were born, the doctor came into the waiting area to give me the news. However, the look on his face indicated something had gone wrong. Your mother told me when we arrived at the hospital that something seemed wrong, although she couldn't precisely say what. The doctor said you were breech, so they had to do a C-section on your mother because the umbilical cord had wrapped itself around your neck and was choking you. I thought he was going to tell me you were dead, son. He said you weren't out of the woods yet, but he predicted they would release you in a few days. And you were. You were a fighter —inherited that from your mother.

But then the doctor told me to sit down, that he had some bad news. That's when he told me that your dear mother had lost too much blood and that she had died. I was devastated, and honestly, this is the first moment of clarity that I've had since, if indeed I am thinking clearly. The world lost an exceptional woman in your mother. You lost a mother. I lost a wife. Neither one of us has much family left to speak of, but the church lost a faithful member, and the ladies on our street lost a loving friend. She was full of life and joy, your mother. She would have made a tremendous mother, too—I'm sure of it.

But it was not to be. That has been the story of my life, son, a characteristic I hope I haven't passed along to you. Life has snatched hope from me more times than I can count, but this one is by far the worst, and I don't see any coming back from it. I am helpless in caring for you. I tried but my heart is not it. That doesn't mean I don't love you with all my heart. You and probably everyone else will say I quit and took the coward's way out, but there is nothing easy about what I'm going through right now. I know I can't provide everything you're going to need to live a better life than the one I've lived. I'm too old to marry someone who could take care of you, and I can't imagine being married to anyone but your mother, anyway.

If the people who receive this letter follow my instructions, you will read it for the first time after your eighteenth birthday but not actually on your birthday. You'll be too young to feel my death as I write this letter, but it might devastate you if I left this as some type of evil eighteenth birthday gift. Son, I love you too much to do that to you. I don't know what will happen to you after today, but I trust someone will take good care of you and that you grow up to be great at whatever you choose to do. I hope you marry early and have healthy children without the problems your mother and I encountered. A few dollars and the family name is all I have to leave you, for what the family name is worth. I hope you will be the one to remove the curse that seems to rest on it.

Love, Dad (Larry Perdue)

———

DAVID SUCKED IN A LONG, deliberate breath. "Mr. Perdue, again, I'm at a loss for words. I'm so sorry this happened to you."

"This is the third or fourth copy of this letter. I've worn the other ones out, picking apart every sentence, every phrase, every word, trying to understand why my father would give up, why he would leave me for just whoever to raise. He didn't have a plan for me. Like he said in the letter, though, he wasn't thinking clearly after my mother died. The letter seems lucid enough and even well crafted, but I can feel his pain and loneliness and hopelessness in every sentence. He wrote that I was too young to feel his death, and perhaps I was, but I can tell you I have carried his death as far back as I can remember.

"I can't recall when I figured it out, but I started asking questions pretty early. I doubt she was supposed to, but one of my foster mothers told me my mother died giving birth to me and that my father died about two weeks later. When I asked her how he died, she clammed up. I created scenarios over the next few years that had him dying in a car wreck or an accident at work or from a sudden illness. My best one had him passing away in his sleep with a broken heart. Deep inside, though, I think I understood he took his own life.

"When I aged out of the system at eighteen, my case worker gave me Dad's letter with some other paperwork. She told me my dad didn't want me to open the letter on my birthday and she thought it was best to give it a few days or a week before I opened it. Of course, if you tell a teenager he can't do something, what's going to happen?"

"You opened the letter."

"As soon as she drove away. To tell you the truth, it was good for me to read it. It answered a lot of my questions, and it confirmed my suspicion that my father committed suicide. It became comforting for me to know that he died in his sleep of a broken heart—in a manner of speaking—at least at first. Over the years as I have researched my family history, I have felt sorry for him, been angry at him, and dealt with bitterness because of him. During some of my low points, I have blamed him for everything wrong with my life. Ultimately, though, I came to understand and forgive him."

"Wow. My mom has gone through all those things with my dad, and I guess my sister and I have, too, to a lesser degree. She only reached forgiveness this year after she committed her life to God. Did you do that, too, Mr. Perdue?"

"I did, but not until a lot of researching my family and learning about my great-grandfather. I met Jesus in college, but at times I have still blamed God for everything that had happened to me and to my parents. It was easy for me to shift the fault to someone, anyone, and God seemed to be a reasonable place to point since I couldn't see him, anyway. When I found out my parents were faithful, active members of their church, that only added fuel to my fire later on."

"What changed your mind?"

"David Gull, my story takes a lot of twists and turns that I would have to explain to make my answer to your question make any sense. And I believe you have a window to replace." When David's face registered disappointment, Perdue said, "Unless you don't mind an old man looking over your shoulder and rattling on about his life while you work."

"No, sir, I would consider it an honor." Rising to his feet and reaching for his tool bag, David stopped. "Mr. Perdue, you don't know me from Adam. If you don't mind my asking, what would make you trust me with your story?"

Perdue scratched his head full of more-salt-than-pepper hair. "I don't know. Maybe because you seemed conscientious. I saw you at the door five minutes early this morning, and that sets you apart from your generation right there. You're twenty-two, the owner of a successful company, and here on Thanksgiving to take care of a problem you didn't create. I thought to myself, I could trust somebody like that. Then, when you listened like you weren't in a hurry to get to your work, I decided to keep going until you acted like you had heard enough. But you haven't, and I appreciate that. Plus, telling my story out loud helps me know if my book is worth publishing."

"No question about that. I'll buy the first copy."

"Young fella, I'm just getting started good. You must make me a promise, though."

"Yes, sir, what?"

"Don't repeat it to the staff here. Or anybody else, for that matter. Make them buy the book."

"I've already given you my word on that, and my word is my bond. Let's go take care of your window and get on to the next chapter of your story."

5

"Let me show you something before you get started, David." Perdue pushed aside the cardboard that had covered the inside of his window and motioned for David to step in front of the window. "Tell me what you see."

"A broken window."

"Look harder."

"A spider web."

"Keep looking."

"A window that's broken on one side but not the other. Is that what you're aiming for?"

"Now we're getting somewhere. What else?"

"Broken on the outside, but not inside?" When Perdue didn't answer, David mulled over his words. *Broken on the outside, but not inside. Seems like there's a life lesson in there somewhere. What's he getting at?* "Help me out, Mr. Perdue."

"Kinda pretty from the inside, isn't it?"

"I suppose so. Yeah, it kinda is, but you can't see through it clearly. Might make for an interesting photograph for someone who knows something about photography."

"You just said a mouthful there, David. Now, consider why you're here today."

"Because one of my guys sent a rock crashing into your window, and I want to replace your old window with a new one. Am I getting warm?"

"Warmer. Be more specific."

David thought for a long time, scanning back and forth between the window and his curious new friend. "Because one of my guys broke your window on the outside?"

"That's right," Perdue said, excited this young man was following his trail of bread crumbs. "If someone had broken the window on the inside, you wouldn't have been here today. You would have never even known it was broken, and it wouldn't have been your responsibility to repair it if you had known. Think about it, David. In a couple of hours, some group—probably from a church or school—will show up in the dining hall with Thanksgiving meals for all us old folks. Why do you think that is?"

"Because they want to serve? Or maybe they just want to help? If they're from a school, they might be fulfilling service hours."

"By serving the needy? You tasted the coffee in there. Our food is just as appetizing because we're the fortunate seniors who can afford the absolute best care. No one here is financially needy. If that's true, why do the volunteers insist on coming? It's okay to be brutally honest. You won't hurt my feelings."

"I guess people might assume old people who live in a retirement home are inherently lonely. Whoever arranged their coming here may have thought a few hours of their time might mean something to those of you who live here."

"Bingo. I see things differently because I wasn't raised in what you might call a normal family, but we seniors have more community here than most people out there in the so-called real world do. But people from the outside assume I'm lonely because I fit the profile—my outside pane is broken, so to speak. What they can't see is that my figurative inside pane is just fine. And they'll be too focused on doing busywork like passing out plates and cleaning up after us that they won't make much of an effort to see my inner pane, you might say. My inner pane hasn't always been fine, though. For most of my life, I lived with a distorted pane on the inside while my outside pane didn't look much different from any other healthy person's."

"I think I get it," David said. "This doubled-paned window is a symbol for the emotional pain that people either feel or that the world assumes they are experiencing."

"Right, but how often have you seen one of these windows broken through both panes?"

"None that I can remember."

"That's right, and why is that?"

"Because the manufacturer creates each pane to take

the force of a blow—like a rock slung from a mower—
without damaging the other one."

"For sure. And you are only truly affected by the
damage on your side, whether that's from the inside or
the outside. I'm sure your worker thought a lot more
about the damage he had caused to my window than I
did because the damage on his side was considerable. I
could see the broken pane from my side, but I was unaf-
fected by it. Other than not being able to see the world
clearly because of something somebody had done to my
window—even though it was unintentional—it didn't
bother me. I was in no danger of glass falling out and
cutting me. Actually, I enjoyed the beauty of the spider
web through the clear pane on my side. That's why you
found your guy's cardboard on my floor this morning.
Is this clicking with you, my young friend?"

"Yes, sir, it sure is, and I can see why you told the
lady at the front desk not to cover it up again. You're a
deep thinker, Mr. Perdue."

"Years of perspective, son, learned from the side of
the broken pane. I'm hoping that telling my story can
help someone who is where I was for so many years
clean up his glass and replace his inner pane with an
unbroken one sooner than I did. Then, David, all of my
effort will be worth it."

"Yes, sir, I think you're right. Are you ready for me to
get started on your window so you can see clearly through
both panes again? Or would you rather I call a photogra-
pher to come over and document your experience?"

"No need. I took pictures this morning to inspire me

while I'm writing. I hope you don't mind if I take a few while you're working."

"No problem at all." David grabbed his razor knife to score the paint over the window stops. Before he sliced along the first edge, he turned back to Perdue, who had settled in on the end of his bed to watch. "You know, the glass is tinted, and the gas between the panes is there to provide extra insulation. I'm not sure you can use that in your writing, but those two aspects of the window just crossed my mind, and I thought you might find them interesting."

"That's good, real insightful. I like the way you think." Perdue pulled a notepad and pen from his desk drawer and scribbled some notes while David proceeded with the uninstall. While he worked, Perdue talked.

"My earliest memory is when I was six years old," he began.

"NAME'S PERDUE," one stressed out, overworked social worker said to another. "He's been passed around from home to home already, but nobody wants to keep him for one reason or another. They all say he's a good enough kid—behaves himself but talks too much, asks too many questions."

"Hello, little fella." Social worker number two addressed Hershel Perdue as if he had appeared out of thin air and wasn't privy to the conversation that had just taken place right in front of him. "How are you today?"

Hershel shrugged his shoulders. "Fine." Had he responded with any other adjective, positive or negative, her response would have been the same.

"Mm-hmm. Now, it says here you just had a birthday?"

"Yes."

"Did you have a party? Get any presents?" She should have known those questions were a shot in the dark with a foster kid.

"No." The dejected pall that fell over Hershel's face went as unnoticed as his answer.

"Mm-hmm. Are you excited about going to school next year?"

"I guess. I know my letters, but I would like to learn how to read."

"Mm-hmm, mm-hmm." Setting her pen on the mound of paperwork in front of her, she turned her attention to her diminutive charge. "Hubert, we're going to find you a place to stay for a few days while we find you a new family, don't you worry. Since you'll be starting school this fall, we'll do our best to find you a family that has a child already in school so they can help you know what to do when you start. How does that sound to you?"

"Herschel."

"What?"

"My name is Hershel."

Double-checking her form, Number Two replied, "So it is, so it is—sorry about that, Herschel. Now, why don't you take your bag and move into the play area in the other room while we work on where you're going to stay tonight."

For the next three hours, Herschel played with blocks, mechanically stacking them up and tearing them down. His outer actions appeared calm and controlled. The voices raging in his head were not so pleasant. *See, nobody wants you.* My mama wanted me. *Your daddy didn't.* My mama died, but she wanted me. *Nobody wants you now. Nobody can even remember your name.* My mama would have. *But she's not here and everybody else has forgotten about you.*

"Little boy? Young man? Perdue, is it?"

Herschel shook himself back into the real world. "Perdue, yes, that's me."

"Honey, are you hungry?"

"Yes."

"If you'll come with me, dear, I'll fix you something to eat." Social Worker Number Three seemed nicer than the others. A distinctive Southern accent accompanied her Southern hospitality. She made him a peanut butter and strawberry jelly sandwich—his favorite—and sat him at the table in the break room to eat it. "You might have to sit up on your knees."

The steel folding chair was hard on his knees, but the sandwich and an apple stifled his hunger. Number Three's kindness quelled the voices in his head. Returning to the blocks after lunch, he whiled away the next hour in silence. The family who would take him home later that afternoon would be the closest semblance of a family he would experience for many years.

NUMBER THREE TAPPED Herschel on the shoulder while he was building at least his hundredth tower of the day. "Sweetie, I have somebody I'd like you to meet." Herschel was quick to his feet, standing ramrod straight to present himself for inspection. "Herschel, this is Mrs. Peggy Dunbar. You're going to be staying with her family while we try to find you a new home, okay?"

"Yes, ma'am."

Peggy Dunbar was pretty and smelled like some type of flower that Herschel would recognize much later in life as a gardenia. There was a kindness in her green eyes that he had not seen in any of his other foster parents. "Nice to meet you," he said obligingly, holding his little hand out to shake hers.

"Such good manners. Your name is Herschel?"

"Yes, ma'am."

"That's an interesting name. Well, Herschel, I have two boys about your age. They like playing with blocks, too. Maybe you will enjoy playing with them."

"Don't forget your bag, sweetie," Number Three intervened. "Let's get you going." He grabbed his paper sack and followed Peggy Dunbar to her waiting car.

DAVID HAD the window ready to pull from its casing, but he didn't want to interrupt Perdue's story. "Sounds like a beneficial situation for you. What happened?"

"What I didn't know then was that there were families in the foster care system who took care of kids like me who were between homes. They weren't looking to adopt, but they helped by taking emergency placements. Mrs. Peggy had been a social worker for a few years before she married and had children, so she had a soft spot for us kids who got passed around from house to house.

"Her boys were a year older and a year younger than me, and we took to each other right away. They had seen children coming and going through their house as far back as they could remember, so they took my coming to them in stride. I was there for a night. Then two. Then a week. Now, recall that I didn't understand what the Dunbars' role was; I just went wherever the people at child services instructed me to go. One night, though, when I was in the hall bathroom pretending to wash my hands before supper, I heard the Dunbar boys asking their parents if they could keep me. Looking back, I would have understood more about my circumstances if I had waited for an answer. I was already walking back toward the kitchen, and Mr. Dunbar glanced in my direction before he answered their question. When he saw me, he clammed up. That's the last they said about my staying within my earshot.

"I guess it was about two weeks later, though, that they replaced my pallet on the boys' floor with a bed. Tommy and Nathan were in bunk beds, so there was enough space. Again, I was six years old, so I didn't process that change like I might have. I started school still living with the Dunbars. Tommy and Nathan introduced me as their little brother, even though I was a year older than Nathan, so I went along with it. It wasn't until later in the year when our class parties and plays and things like that began that I realized how unusual my life was. Everybody else in the class seemed to have a normal family. While my situation was more advantageous than ever before, it didn't prevent me from feeling like an outcast.

"I think Mrs. Peggy anticipated some of the questions rolling around in my mind because she would tell me these little sayings to encourage me. I can't remember them now, but she would let me know God hadn't forgotten about me. My life might have differed from the other kids, but she claimed it was because He had a special purpose for me. I didn't understand half of what she told me, but it was comforting the way she said it. Plus, when she held me in her lap and rocked me while she talked, I enjoyed her scent. It wasn't until I bought my first home down here in Mississippi and built my landscape that I encountered a gardenia bush for the first time. When that thing bloomed the next summer, I was walking by it one day when I caught a whiff. That aroma transported me back to Mrs. Peggy's front porch, rocking back and forth in her lap and her telling me how special I was to God and to her.

"A few months turned into a year. The Dunbars threw me a birthday party for my seventh birthday—I remember that. Mrs. Peggy let me pick what we ate for supper—I wanted hamburgers and French fries—and she made me a chocolate cake. You could guess what I wished for before I blew out the candles. We ate cake and ice cream, and I told Mrs. Peggy it was the best birthday I had ever had. She laughed and told me we hadn't even gotten to the presents yet.

"I started with the presents from Tommy and Nathan. Tommy gave me a pack of peppermint sticks like the ones he was always sucking on, and Nathan gave me a pack of the circus peanuts he liked so well. I had never received presents for my birthday before, so I was more than willing to share. Then, Mrs. Peggy pulled out this huge package and told me it was a special gift from her and Mr. Dunbar. I was so excited that I tore into the wrapping like there was no tomorrow. Turns out, tomorrow was all I had left with the Dunbars, but I wasn't aware of it yet. They had bought me a brand new suitcase, a child-sized one with 'Davy Crockett, King of the Wild Frontier' emblazoned on the side.

"Mrs. Peggy said that it could replace the paper bag I carried my clothes in when I came to stay with them. One of the most vivid memories I have is throwing my arms around that suitcase and holding onto it for the longest time. I felt a sense of belonging unlike any I had ever had in my life. Then, when I let go of the suitcase, I asked Mrs. Peggy if we were going somewhere. When everybody froze, I understood. I have a way of undercutting my own birthdays, it seems. They didn't want to tell me until the next day, but Mr. Dunbar's job was transferring him to California, and I wouldn't be going with them. I was still a ward of the state of Michigan.

"It must have broken Mrs. Peggy's heart when I looked up at her with tears in my eyes and asked if I could keep the suitcase. She hugged me as hard as I had hugged that suitcase and told me it was mine forever and forever and that she was so sorry they were having to move away from me. I returned her hug and told her I would never forget her. She held me an extra long time on the front porch swing that night. Saying goodbye the following morning was excruciating, but by the next afternoon, I was back to building block towers in the child services office, off to the next of many more homes over the next eleven years."

6

David sighed. "I hate to keep saying I'm sorry, Mr. Perdue, so how about this: You must have built up quite a resilience in those years."

"That's right, my boy, you are correct. I wish I had started then counting how many homes I stayed in for at least a night—it had to be at least twenty. Thing is, I was never a problem child like some other foster children who found themselves adopted. If you were to write a description of an adoptable child, I was it, but it just never worked out for one reason or the other. I sometimes wonder how my life might have turned out if the Dunbars had adopted me, and I had grown up with them.

"I didn't stay anywhere more than a year until high school. The only constant was my Davy Crockett, King of the Wild Frontier suitcase. Other children in the houses where I lived, especially if they were foster kids, picked at me because of it, but I didn't care. It was a link to the last person I felt like loved me. Mrs. Peggy was one of the few people I met before college whom I could point to and say they loved me, but I always believed my mother loved me, too. Again, I can't rightly say why no one ever adopted me. I wouldn't have wanted to be adopted by most of my foster families, but surely someone had room for a low-maintenance kid like me.

"All the while, though, I loved to learn. That didn't mean I always loved school; I mean, kids and adults can be cruel to an orphan. I've never understood that, especially why even a few of my teachers picked at me for something so out of my control. Through the years, I have often wondered if it made other kids feel better about themselves to be mean to me. Maybe they were frightened somehow of the unknown, or, perhaps by chance or purpose, I just encountered a string of cruel people. If left alone to my studies, I made excellent grades and enjoyed school. That usually wasn't the case, but there always seemed to be at least one teacher and sometimes a classmate who encouraged me and kept me pushing forward. Even with my difficulties with school, I read books like there was no tomorrow, and I paid attention to the way people did things.

"When I was a teenager, I moved to a group home for boys, where I lived from ninth grade until I aged out of the system. The other boys razzed me about the suitcase when I arrived—it was pretty outdated and childish by then—but other than that, life at the boys' home wasn't too bad. All of us had our different issues since most of us were on the path to aging out before anyone adopted us. We might have been the bottom of the barrel of society, but at least we didn't have to feel like we were facing the world alone.

"There were a group of seven of us a grade or two apart in school who stayed together for a few years. We were pretty tight-knit, but we didn't open up much to outsiders. We had our house parents, the Huffigans, and two other families who would give them a break on the weekends sometimes, but our house parents also brought in people to teach us a variety of things. That was positive because it helped some of us find our place during high school and gave us some know-how to help us find a career after we aged out. After two high school coaches came out to spend some time with us one summer, two of the guys a year ahead of me signed up to play football. One of them even earned a football scholarship to college, which none of us could afford. Another time, this farmer came out to teach us how to grow food, and he helped us plant a garden for our boys' home. That was a lot of work, but we learned some useful skills.

"Most people who came to help us were there to fulfill a project for college or some club or church group that set it up. People who have been rejected most of their lives can detect when people are genuine about spending time with them and when they're faking it. Like you, David. I wouldn't be telling you my life story if I didn't read you as someone who truly wanted to know it. Am I right?"

"Yes, sir, for sure."

"As I look back on it, one of the most significant days of my life was when Mr. Mitchell came out to the home one Saturday morning. He wasn't there to represent anybody, just wanted to help. After talking to our house parents at church one Sunday—you know, asking them questions about the boys' home and all—he set up a day to visit. Mr. Mitchell was an older guy who had been a carpenter most of his life. He had just sold his cabinet business and was picking up various odd jobs to stay busy, so he was semi-retired, I guess you'd say. He brought his tools and some one-by-six boards to teach us how to make bluebird houses.

"Mr. Mitchell was a real soft-spoken man with skin the color of coffee with just a hint of creamer, and two guys in the back started making fun of him when he was going through the safety procedures before plugging in his tools. He kind of stopped what he was doing and casually asked the troublemakers what they normally did on Saturday morning. They snickered and told him if he hadn't come, they would still be sleeping. He nodded and told us he understood if we wanted to leave and do something else, that we wouldn't hurt his feelings at all. Well, the two clowns in the back started walking away and urged the rest of us to join them. Some of the the boys walked inside with them and went back to bed, and others left to continue putting together a puzzle they had started the previous evening. Five minutes after Mr. Mitchell freed us to leave it we wanted, only he and I were left.

"Don't you want to leave, too, son? Seriously, it won't bother me if you want to work the puzzle with the others or go back to bed. It won't bother me a bit."

"If it's okay with you, I think I'd like to stay. I've always liked to build things, but nobody has ever taught me how to use tools, especially power tools."

Mr. Mitchell smiled. "That's why I'm here, young man, even if it's just you and me. What's your name?"

"Herschel Perdue."

"Well, Perdue, let's start with a birdhouse today, and see what you've got. If you want to learn to build other things after that, I'll be glad to help you."

By the time the house parents rang the bell for lunch, Herschel and Mr. Mitchell had produced six bluebird houses, each one better than the last. Herschel watched on the first one, made his first tentative cut on the second one, and was doing all the work under Mr. Mitchell's supervision by birdhouse number four. He held up his last one to his teacher, satisfied he had built it to Mr. Mitchell's specifications.

"That's mighty fine work."

"For a beginner?"

"For anybody. Perdue, what do you plan to do with all these birdhouses?"

"I don't know. Nail them to the trees outside my window, I guess. Would it be okay if kept one in my room as a way to remember learning to make these today?"

"They're yours to do what you want to with them. I'm glad you're going to use most of them as they were intended, though. Be a shame to withhold such well-crafted accommodations from the birds. What grade are you in, Perdue?"

"Ninth."

"You picked up basic carpentry pretty quickly for a boy your age. If you think you want to learn some more carpentry, you tell Mr. Huffigan, and I'll be glad to come back and teach you how to make other things."

"Mr. Mitchell?"

"Yep."

"What if I already know?"

"Know what, Perdue?"

"That I want you to teach me more about building things. I would like to learn to use other tools if you wouldn't mind teaching me."

"All right, all right, Perdue. There you go—eliminate the middleman. I like it, I like it. Tell you what, you be thinking about what you want to build next, and I'll be in touch with Huffigan. Now, the job's not finished until you clean up, so do your part by putting the tools in the back of my truck. It's the bright yellow one out front—can't miss it."

Herschel hustled the tools out to the truck and was back before Mr. Mitchell had finished sweeping the shop floor. "Mr. Mitchell?"

"Yep."

"I already know."

"Know what, Perdue?"

"What I want to build next."

"All right, all right. So tell me what you have in mind for your next project."

"A porch swing. The one on our front porch has been

broken since I arrived here, and I think I would like to make one to replace it. All the boys could use it, even if they were rude and didn't stick around for your wood-working lesson today."

"That's okay, Perdue. Gave us more one-on-one time to discover your hidden talents. A porch swing, huh? Tell you what, let's take some measurements and see if we can't build you boys a swing next time." More to himself, he muttered, "Seems like most of them would rather sit around than work, anyway."

"Two weeks later, sitting on the swing that I made—well, I did most of the work—I had the idea for my first business. When Mr. Mitchell came back out a few weeks later, I had an outline of a business plan ready for him. We would make swings together and sell them until I could afford to buy my own equipment, and then I would make them by myself. He laughed at me—not like I was used to other people laughing at me. His was more because I already had a plan to cut him out of the business that he hadn't agreed to start yet. Mr. Mitchell had a novel idea, though. He would help me gather some good equipment if my house parents said it was okay, and he would split the profit fifty-fifty if I would do all the work and let him supervise. He would let me cut him out only if I agreed to come to work for him during my breaks from school.

"Well, shoot, that was a win-win proposition for me. I could make money on my business and get paid while he was teaching me on the job. Mr. Mitchell wasn't just helping me out because he felt sorry for me, either. You know how I could tell?"

David was so engrossed in Perdue's story that several seconds of silence passed before he realized an answer was required. "Because he stayed when only you wanted to learn?"

"No, I knew he was serious when he took his share of the proceeds of our swing sales. He didn't need the money. It would have been easy enough for him to repay himself for the materials that it took to build the swing and let me have the rest. That wouldn't have taught me the true value of work, though, would it? At least Mr. Mitchell didn't think so. By the end of the school year, we had sold five or six swings, enough for me to have enough money to buy some suitable tools. That's when Mr. Mitchell said he knew I was serious, when I invested that pile of money I had saved into the tools I needed to keep going on my own. He found some quality used equipment to save me some money and took me to the hardware store for the rest. When we were leaving the store after buying everything else I needed, he looked down at me and said, 'None of them sleeping boys would have turned loose of that much money like you just did, Perdue. I'm proud of you. Proud of you.'"

David grinned. "I bet that meant a lot to you."

"It did, for sure. I couldn't recollect any grownup ever having said it to me before he did."

"What was it like working for Mr. Mitchell during your summers?"

Perdue's face turned downcast. "Never found out. He dropped dead of a massive heart attack two weeks before school was out at the end of my freshman year of high school."

"You've got to be kidding me."

"That's the story of at least two generations of Perdues right there, David. Like my dad's life, I never could keep any traction my efforts generated. Don't feel sorry for me, though. You keep listening—you'll find out my time's coming. Even then, no matter how life soured for me, there were three things I carried with me: my mama wanted me, Mrs. Peggy loved me, and Mr. Mitchell was proud of me."

7

"I need to walk outside to get the other window out of my truck," David said, leaning the broken window backward to pull it from the frame. "You can walk with me if you'd like and continue your story."

"If you don't mind the company."

"Are you kidding? Your story is fascinating, Mr. Perdue."

"All right, let's go."

David noticed the dining hall stirring with preparation for the Winding Acres Thanksgiving meal. Just as Perdue had predicted, students from one of the local high schools—all dressed in their identical navy blue, red, and white T-shirts scurried about. While they arranged plastic cornucopia centerpieces and place settings on all the tables, David noticed the clock on the wall behind the receptionist's station read 10:15. Had he been talking to Perdue for over two hours already? The time was flying, but the older man's story had him hooked.

WHEN THE UNLIKELY companions reached David's truck, the young entrepreneur tossed the broken window into the bed of the truck. "The new window is in the back-seat. I'll get it, and we can get you fixed up."

Perdue was staring at the tailgate of the work truck. "That's a nice logo you have there."

"You like it?"

"Yeah, it's simple, but unique. I like that your logo shows more of the roots than the grass. Does that have some kind of symbolism, or am I reading too much into it?"

"When I was doing my second tour in Iraq, we had a lot of downtime. One of my Army buddies was a whiz at graphic design, so we started tinkering with a logo for my company back home. We were two of the only guys in our unit who didn't drink or smoke, so we found it an interesting way to pass the time. I was all set to call my company *Grass Roots,* so my buddy helped me design this logo.

"I kept it a secret from the guys doing all the lawn work while I was away. When I came back and told them about my plans to grow the company, including the new name, they were excited about it at first. Then one of them lingered after our reveal meeting. I asked him what was wrong, and he said something that changed the course of my thinking about my company.

"I could tell Whit had been listening and taking notes during our meeting. He showed me a flow chart on his notepad with a crude copy of the logo, the vision I had laid out for the company, and some keywords I had repeated through the years. He said, 'David, I like the logo, but I'm not sold on the name. You built this company from the ground up, so you tied the company's reputation to your name. I appreciate that you're too humble to want to take all the glory for our success, but I think doing away with your name as the company's name would be a mistake. Perhaps you should take some time to rethink that decision.'

"We argued back and forth for a little while because a major part of my vision for the company is to empower my associates. The only time this company revolved around me is when I was the sole proprietor. The day I hired my first employee—and I hate using that term—my passion has been to make them better in every area of their lives I can touch. I thought that a move to a company name that didn't include mine would excite the guys, but Whit made some good points. We volleyed back and forth for a while until he said, 'Why don't you call the company Gull & Associates, keep the logo, and add the tagline *Grass Roots Groundskeeping*?' So I did.

"I felt better about including my hardworking guys in the company name while keeping the grass roots part. The double meaning is that we built the company from the ground up. Whit explained it to the rest of the guys the following day. They loved it, and we haven't looked back. I have been able to go back to our core values pretty often in talking to my guys, especially new associates, and in talking to potential clients about our company. Sorry, that was a long answer to a short question, but thanks for asking, anyway."

"You continue to surprise me, young David Gull. Sounds like this Whit fellow has a knack for business and marketing. You'd better do everything you can to keep him around."

"He became my first account manager this year. He has been loyal to me, especially when I was overseas, and I love being able to reward somebody like him. Right now, he's working himself through business school, and I have big plans for him if our company continues on the path we're on right now."

"Just curious—how old is Whit?"

"Couple of years older than I am, twenty-four. No, we ordered him a cake last month, and I remember the 25 in the middle having the design and colors of his favorite race car driver."

"Hmm."

Something about the look in Perdue's eyes caught David's attention. He locked it away in his memory. For now, he wanted to return to this man's extraordinary story. "Ready for a new window, Mr. Perdue?"

"Let's do it." The two walked back toward the entrance to Winding Acres.

"So, you left off with Mr. Mitchell's death."

"Right. That was right at the end of my freshman year of high school. I went to his funeral—my house parents dropped me off while they ran some errands. They couldn't do that now, and it probably wasn't wise then, but they did. It was the first funeral I had ever attended, so I didn't know how to act. After everything was over, I walked up to Mrs. Mitchell, even though I had never met her or talked to her. I had no idea what to say, but I couldn't walk out without telling her how much her husband meant to me."

"Mrs. Mitchell?"

"Yes?"

"Uh… you… I…"

"It's okay, honey. What's your name?"

Herschel straightened. "My name is Herschel Perdue, ma'am."

A flash of recognition. "You were my husband's business partner, weren't you? You're the young man who put him out of business by working circles around him."

Herschel's head dropped.

"No, honey, that was a little joke. My husband thought the world of you, Perdue. He couldn't stop talking about the business savvy of his little freshman partner and how skilled you are at making things. Trust me, young man, my husband had big plans for teaching and training you."

"I wish I had been able to work for him this summer. I'm going to miss him a lot. He was a real talented carpenter."

"Oh, that he was. More than that, honey, he was a fine man, a fine husband, and a fine father and grandfather. The world lost a good one in my Vernon, and I'm not sure what we'll do without him." Mrs. Mitchell was overcome with emotion for a minute, but she powered through to say what she needed to say to her husband's young protégé. "Perdue, I want you to come by the house sometime this week, if you can. I know my husband would never give away any of his tools because he thought that something given too easily wouldn't be appreciated. I'm going to honor that, but I tell you what I'll do: I'm going to give you some good deals on his best stuff, if you're interested."

"Oh, yes, ma'am, I'm very interested. He was... like you said... a fine man, and I'm sad he died. I'll get Mr. Huffigan—he's my house father—to call you this week and bring me over to look at Mr. Mitchell's tools. I'll bring my money."

"You don't worry about anybody buying anything out from under you, Perdue. If there's anything you see that you want, you just let me know and pay for things as you can. You plan on staying awhile at my house when you come, though, okay? It'll be awfully lonely without Vernon around the house, even though he was gone helping folks most days. You can work in his shop out back and keep your equipment there, too, unless you have a better place for it. Will you do that for a lonely widow woman, Perdue?"

"I JUMPED AT THE OPPORTUNITY. Like her husband, she made me an offer slanted a great deal toward benefitting me in the long run. I visited her that week and pretty much every week after that until I left for college. She would tell me more about Mr. Mitchell and herself, and she was very interested in the life I had led.

"Mrs. Mitchell sold me those tools dirt cheap, but she didn't give them to me. I kept making swings and selling them, even started giving a part of the profit back to the church organization that was the parent charity for our group home. By the time I turned sixteen the next school year, I had saved up enough to buy a truck. I saw a truck as the next level for my little business—you know, selling swings at crafts fairs and church bazaars and places like that. I had been discussing it with Mrs. Mitchell for a while, just asking for her opinion so I didn't make a mistake that would cost me my forward financial momentum. What I didn't know was that she had been saving Mr. Mitchell's yellow pickup truck for me.

She didn't give it to me—that would have gone against how he operated—but she sold it to me for three hundred dollars, which was a far cry less than it was worth. Plus, it still carried his smell, which was priceless to both of us. Even after I bought it from her, we would sometimes sit in it without saying a word but enjoy soaking up the aroma of the intersection of man, tools, and the sawdust that was so ingrained in the carpet that it never completely came out. Not that I tried too hard to remove it.

"One thing Mrs. Mitchell kept encouraging me to do was to go to college. She would say, 'Perdue, you're good with your hands, but you also have a sharp mind.

You'll make a better living for yourself if you combine the two.' If she said that once, she said it a hundred times. I started dreaming about going to college not long after I started visiting with her.

"David, not too long ago, I looked at the statistics about foster kids going to college, and they're staggering. There are plenty of kids in the system who say they want to attend college, but a quarter of them never finish high school. Only about three percent will ever earn a college degree, and that's by today's numbers. You can imagine the numbers were stacked even more against a foster kid in 1971, when I graduated from high school."

David jiggled the replacement window into place. He turned to where Perdue had returned to his post at the end of his bed and trained his phone's camera on David.

"Did you go?"

"Indeed, I did, but that's a story in itself, if you have time to listen to it."

"I don't have any plans until tonight. I'm going with my mom to a reunion with a group of people she met two years ago on Thanksgiving. Last year, they met again and included all the families. It was pretty cool, and I don't want to miss it. Plus, there's—promise you won't repeat it if I tell you a secret?"

"On my word as a gentleman," Perdue answered, solemnly holding up his right hand to pledge his fidelity.

David smiled. "The girl who started their little group —she's pretty awesome and as of the last time I saw her a couple of months ago, still unattached. She's older than me, but I figure I'm twenty-two now and… who knows, right? Maybe that won't seem so young to her."

"Young man, if she's looking at your biological age, you might seem young, but if you're going by maturity, she would be a fool not to at least give you a shot." That comment sat in the air for a few seconds. "Mr. David Gull, I do believe you're blushing. Are you smitten with this young lady?"

"So… about your window," David said, grasping for a new topic. "Like it?"

"Sure, it looks great. We can talk about something else if you're embarrassed."

"That would be great. How about the next chapter of your story?"

"Still interested, are you? This is trending well for my book."

"You have me hooked. I need to add some weather stripping to your window to be finished, but I'm sticking around for the story. That should tell you something. You should do an audiobook, too. I think people would love to hear you tell your story."

"All right, here goes 'Perdue: The College Years.' That's my working chapter title."

8

"Perdue, you have mail!" Mr. Huffigan shouted above the din of the paper football tournament that dominated the rainy early November day in the common area of the boys' home. He held three letters aloft as the boys created a lane for Herschel to collect his latest college correspondence.

Herschel's college journey had long been a source of fascination for the boys in the home. Since deciding he wanted to pursue a college degree, he had written hundreds of colleges for information packets. Dozens of applications all over the country followed between his junior and senior years of high school after he culled his choices to just under a hundred. The acceptance and rejection letters were an almost daily occurrence now. He tore into the first of this round, scanning for the bottom line to announce the verdict to the rest of the guys. They gathered near the large chalkboard in the common room, where Herschel's current options were listed.

"Okay, here we go," he began. "Fort Hays State says yes. Put them on the board."

"Where's that?" asked Mr. Huffigan a lifelong Michigan resident who had earned his degree in social work from Michigan State and was rooting for the Spartans in his charge's college quest. "I've never even heard of Fort Hays State."

"It's in Hays, Kansas, in the northwestern part of the state. I don't even remember applying there." Herschel enjoyed the geography lessons he was often called upon to give when letters arrived from far reaches of the country.

"How many stars for Fort Hays State?" asked the chalkboard scribe. Herschel ranked each college to which he had been accepted with three stars for *firm possibility*, two for *strong consideration*, and one for *not likely*.

"Since I don't even remember applying there, give them one star for now." The star system, he knew, would change when he reached the critical juncture of applying for financial aid. He felt it worth the investment to spend now on correspondence and application fees, hoping to win scholarships later, which would be the biggest determining factor in his choosing the right school. His grades weren't at the top of his class, but he hoped that his good grades in the face of the personal adversity he had faced and his personal business experience would win the day when scholarship committees considered his applications.

"Who's next?" asked the scribe.

"Winthrop University—Rock Hill, South Carolina." Herschel opened the envelope, scanned the letter, and announced, "Wait list. I figured Winthrop was a long shot. Oh, well, South Carolina might have been nice."

One of the younger residents piped up, "Perdue, would you travel that far away from home to go to college?"

"What home are you talking about? This one?" The boy tucked his head sheepishly into his shoulder. Herschel continued, "I don't mean any disrespect to you guys or to the Huffigans. These past four years have been the most stable years of my life, but once I age out, I have nowhere to go home to—no grandparents, aunts, uncles, just me. So wherever I go to college, I'll be building my life there and then wherever my studies or internships take me from there. If that's in Michigan, fine, but there is nothing and nobody keeping me here. I wish you guys the best, but you'll all be going your separate ways, too."

His words sank into the souls of the juniors and seniors in the room. The statistics said that a significant number of them would end up in jail within a few years of their aging out of the foster care system. Half of them would struggle with alcoholism. Perdue was their best hope of producing a college graduate, and the crew of seven near his age saw him as their champion. His lofty hopes and dreams helped fuel their lesser ones.

"Last one, Purdue University—West Lafayette, Indiana."

"Let's put that one on the board before he opens the

letter," the scribe quipped. "They've got to take you, right, Perdue? You can tell 'em your ancestor started the school, so they have to admit you and for free, too."

"If I did that, I'd have to explain why I spell my name differently than the school's. Okay... Purdue is a... no." Herschel dropped the hand that held the letter, disappointed. "I knew their acceptance rate was pretty low, but I was hoping—maybe because of the name thing—that perhaps they would give me a shot. Well, that's it for today's episode of *Where Is Herschel Going to College*. We now return you to your regularly scheduled paper football tournament."

The rest of the boys scurried back to the breakfast table for the semifinals of the tournament. Herschel walked to the chalkboard to review his options. Fort Hays State in Kansas made eight possible destinations so far. He had given Michigan State three stars because they were the closest, but the Spartans hadn't captured his interest. Butler University in Indianapolis and Tulane University in New Orleans also earned three stars, but they were also the priciest. The school that kept catching his eye was Millsaps College in Jackson, Mississippi. It was an expensive private school, but not as pricy as the other private three-star options. Even though he had worked hard and saved well from his porch swing business, he would still need plenty of financial assistance to earn his college degree. Whatever it took, Perdue determined to make it happen.

As THE ACADEMIC calendar turned from fall to spring, Herschel's list of acceptances stood at twelve. After receiving the financial aid offer from each of the schools on his list, he had the scribe draw a line through the colleges that were out of his financial reach. He would place a box around those still in the running for his acceptance. Only two colleges remained unmarked.

One day in early March, the boys gathered in the den to watch television after school when Mr. Huffigan walked in with the daily mail. "Perdue, two more letters today!" These would be the final two and determine his legitimate college choices.

Herschel took the letters from his house father with more apprehension than he had received the acceptance letters. Mr. Huffigan and the boys took their places in the common area for Perdue's almost daily routine of narrowing his choices. The annotated board revealed his dwindling options. He had eliminated Butler and DePaul and five others he couldn't afford. Michigan State and Fort Hays State offered enough financial aid to remain realistic choices. East Carolina was a borderline option, though he would have to work his way through school to afford it. Millsaps College in Jackson, Mississippi, and Otterbein University in Westerville, Ohio, were the last two schools on the board from whom he had not heard before today.

"Otterbein first," he announced. As he read, his lips parted in a smile. "Pretty good money, full tuition scholarship, plus books, no room and board. Not bad, not bad at all. Draw a box around it. Right up there with Michigan State for number one. Now, Millsaps."

Herschel read the letter, then read it again before announcing, "Wow, guys, Millsaps has offered me a full scholarship, including room and board. I would be responsible for books and incidentals, that's all."

"Yeah, wouldn't you spend a lot of money on travel?" the scribe asked.

"Remember, travel is one way, one time," Herschel said. "Once I'm there, I will live there until I graduate, maybe longer if that's where I decide to stay and work."

"Oh, that's right." The scribe placed the fourth block around *Millsaps College*. "So here are the choices," he said, heralding what everyone in the room could already see: "Michigan State in Michigan, Fort Hays State in Kansas, Otterbein College in Ohio, and Millsaps College in Mississippi." He erased the other eight that had a line drawn through them. "So what's your choice, Herschel? Where are you going? You're braver than I am, even considering moving all the way to Mississippi."

Herschel swelled with a tremendous sense of accomplishment when he looked at the colleges remaining on the board. They wanted him as an undergraduate at their schools, wanted him enough to pay him to come to their schools. "I want to go somewhere smaller, a place where I won't get lost in the crowd. Erase Michigan State. Consider them third place." The crowd in the common area groaned as the local favorite was the first eliminated. "Fort Hays made a good run, too, but I don't think it's the school for me. They finished in fourth place." Only Otterbein and Millsaps remained.

Herschel heard someone right behind him whisper,

"There's no way he's going to college in Jackson, Mississippi. It's another world in the South."

"I WAS LEANING toward Millsaps anyway, but when I heard that kid say that, it was like he had thrown down a challenge. I had done a little research about Jackson, Mississippi, in the early '70s. They were just eight years past sit-ins in downtown Jackson, near where the school is. The three civil rights workers were killed eighty miles away in Neshoba County just seven years earlier. Even though I'm white, the thought of moving to a place with that much racial tension made me a little nervous, but my life to that point had been about facing adversity and overcoming obstacles. When I made the announcement that I chose Millsaps, they didn't believe me at first. I said it again but still didn't convince them, so I marched to the blackboard and erased *Otterbein University* so that just *Millsaps College* was left."

David clapped his hands together softly three times. "Sounds like you were the center of attention at the boys' home your senior year. Circumstances sure seem to have turned around for you by the end of high school."

"That's true, but it didn't take but until the end of my first semester of college to remember that I was different in a way I wouldn't be able to change."

"How's that?"

Before Perdue could answer, a pleasant voice over the loudspeaker in the hall announced, "Winding Acres residents, the dining hall is now prepared to receive residents from the east wing for Thanksgiving lunch. West wing residents, we will call for you in about one hour. Again, east wing residents, please come on down to the dining hall for our Thanksgiving lunch."

"Care to join me for Thanksgiving lunch?" Perdue asked.

"Would that be okay?"

"As much as we pay to live in this place, do you think they're going to turn us out for bringing a guest to lunch one day?"

"I suppose not."

"All right, let's eat some turkey."

THEIR PLATES PILED with accouterments of the holiday, Perdue and his guest found an empty table in the back corner of the room. David set his plate and sweet tea on the table first. "Since you're paying, I'm praying, okay?" After he asked a quick blessing over their food, David allowed Perdue to take a few bites before he encouraged the older man to return to his story.

"Well," Perdue continued, wiping his mouth with his cloth napkin, "I aged out of the boys' home a few weeks before summer break was over. I loaded up the few possessions I owned—my tools, a few books, my clothes—"

"In your Davy Crockett suitcase?"

"You better know it. I didn't care what anybody said about it anymore. Mr. Huffigan gave me a hundred dollars, which was a pretty big deal because he couldn't have made much money as a houseparent. Of course, I had some money in the bank from all my work in high school, so I pulled that out, bought a new set of tires for Mr. Mitchell's old truck, and headed south. I had plenty of time, so I made several stops along the way. When it was cool enough at night, I rolled out a sleeping bag and slept in the bed of my truck. Most of the time, though, I would get a cheap motel room with air conditioning, especially the farther south I drove.

"My plan was to find a motel close to the campus when I arrived in Jackson and kind of get the lay of the land, walk the campus and all. I hadn't counted on spending so much money on motels before I started school, plus the alternator on my truck went out in Grenada on the way down. I burned through what I had figured would be my first semester's spending money before I ever stepped into the classroom.

"When I made it to Jackson and walked around the Millsaps campus, I realized I needed to spend some money on new clothes and a nice pair of shoes if I was going to fit in. It was important for me to conform to the norm because, for the first time, I had a chance to blend in with students my age. I would tell my classmates I was from Michigan, share a little about my high school, tell them about my business venture, maybe, and leave out the part about being a foster kid.

"During long walks in downtown Jackson in the weeks before classes started, I practiced my introductions and how I would spin any personal questions other students would ask me. Here's an interesting side note: When I had my alternator replaced in Grenada, the mechanic saw my Michigan tag and asked me what I was doing in Mississippi. I told him I was going to Millsaps in the fall but that I was arriving a few weeks early. He told me about the Sun-n-Sand motor hotel in downtown Jackson. It was a little over a mile from the campus, but they kept free bologna and crackers in the lobby. He figured that was important to a college kid who he assumed was on a budget.

"I'll tell you the truth, I haven't eaten much bologna since my first year of college, but I ate plenty of it that year. The Sun-n-Sand shut down in the early 2000s, but a group tried to save it as a historical landmark. I read earlier this year that the city demolished most of it, but they saved the iconic sign and the meeting space. They say if you were there when the legislature was in session, you could hear all sorts of political gossip. It's rather interesting, don't you think, that the Sun-n-Sand was known for bologna and politics?"

"Sounds rather redundant."

Perdue threw his head back and cackled, drawing the attention of nearby diners. "You hit the nail on the head there, my boy. Mind if I use that line in my book?"

"I'll look forward to reading it."

"Okay, this next part is going to seem like I'm rambling, but it will be important later on in my story. Like I said, I took a lot of walks in every direction from the school. The neighborhoods were tree lined and beautiful back in those days. One particular house about two miles north of the campus fascinated me from the first time I saw it. It was beautiful, but not so different from others on the neighborhood. The yard behind it was deep, like the owners had purchased the lot where their house sat and the one behind it. Their landscaping resembled a series of individual sitting areas from what I could see from the street. When I walked around the block, I could see another empty lot between this house and the one next to it. I observed the landscaping patterns better from the street behind the place, where you could barely see the house.

"It must have taken years for that family to have created such a beautiful, meandering landscape. The kid in me considered it a perfect place to play hide and seek. I had almost walked past the place when I stopped and did a double take. Up in one of the oak trees was a tree house. It was painted brown and blended in with the trees so well that you could hardly tell it was there, but it made me think I had missed a part of my childhood by not having something cool like that. Growing up in a house full of teenaged boys can be fun, but many times, I wanted to get away to someplace more quiet than our front-porch swing to study or to just be alone. I must have stood and stared at that treehouse for several minutes that day.

"That became my favorite walking route, even after I started school. I imagined that yard as a secret door to another universe. However, I noticed there were never any children back there playing. I would see the couple who owned the house out working in their yard from time to time—they were an older couple, probably grandparents—but I never saw kids there, even on the weekend. I thought their grandchildren must live out of town, and the treehouse was something fun for them to do when they came to visit. Only, they never seemed to visit. I kept a running storyline that I would erase and re-write in my mind every day. Perhaps I was practicing being an author even then. I wish I had written all the stories in my head. It could have been a popular series."

Perdue and David picked at their food for a few minutes, both of them eager to return to Perdue's narrative. After two bites of pecan pie, the prospective author tossed his fork and napkin onto his plate and continued.

"PERDUE, you headed back to Michigan for Christmas break?" Chris Littlejohn asked. Chris was the resident assistant on Perdue's floor, a sophomore from Texas who had taken a liking to the resident of Room 431 of McCabe Hall. Perdue's Yankee accent served as a foil to Littlejohn's Texas twang. Littlejohn liked all the residents who made his role as RA easier by not causing trouble, but Perdue was an interesting study, a mystery that intrigued him.

Littlejohn's question was one of many he had attempted in an effort to acquaint himself with the freshman. He had learned his major, his home state, and his hobby of building swings but scant else. Perdue would talk freely enough about his classes and his desire to one day own a business, a goal the two young men shared, but anything past that was like pulling teeth. The more Perdue resisted, the harder Littlejohn pressed.

"No, I'm going to stick around over the break."

"You have family down here?"

"No."

"Staying with someone from school?"

"No."

"Well, then… wait, you weren't planning on staying in the dorm, were you?"

"Why not?"

"Perdue, the dorm closes over Christmas. You can leave your things, but you have to move out until a few days before spring semester. I'm sorry, but you'll have to move out by five o'clock this afternoon. All of us still working here would appreciate earlier than that."

"Oh, I didn't know that."

"Yeah, and just so you know, you have to move out for the summer unless you're staying for summer school. This dorm is not open during the summer anyway, so you'll have to move out, regardless."

"Okay, thanks for the information."

Three steps away, Littlejohn spun around and said, "Say, why wouldn't you drive or fly home to be with your family over Christmas break?"

Perdue was already walking toward his room and disappeared behind his door without an answer.

9

Hundreds of thoughts channeled through Herschel's head as he turned the corner on a long walk. Chief among them was his finances. Even though he had enough money to stay at the Sun-n-Sand over Christmas break, his savings account was dwindling faster than he had planned. He knew Millsaps would provide a stern academic challenge, so he hadn't pursued a job, much to his chagrin as he considered his current circumstances. Summer employment would be necessary to afford to live in Jackson, but he was hoping the money he had saved would carry him until then.

Even as far south as Jackson was, the weather was too cold in mid-December for Herschel to consider sleeping in the bed of his truck. He considered checking out of the dorm and then sneaking back to his room, but he couldn't afford to get in trouble with the school with as much of his expenses as they were paying. He might use most of the rest of his money at the Sun-n-Sand, but at least he wouldn't go hungry. The thought of eating bologna and crackers for another month was less than appealing, but it seemed his best option. He would take his tools and look for the opportunity to make a porch swing or two for someone's Christmas present. When he rounded the corner of his favorite street and strolled past the treehouse lot, another idea dawned.

When Herschel returned from his final exam early Friday afternoon, his roommate had packed and gone. He was halfway to Little Rock by now. The cafeteria would serve its last meal that evening, and Herschel planned to take advantage of his last paid-for meal for the next month.

"Hey, Perdue, you headed out?" Littlejohn called from his door on the other end of the hall.

"Not just yet. I just took my western civ final, so I'm going to pack a few things and then head over to the cafeteria to eat dinner."

"What time do you think you'll check out? I can't leave until everybody on the floor has checked out, and I'd like to get on the road."

"Oh, sorry, I didn't know. I'll hurry." Herschel grabbed his tool bag, his winter clothes, general business textbook, and his sleeping bag and hustled them to his truck, one of only a dozen vehicles left in the parking lot. He returned to the floor so Littlejohn could inspect his room.

The resident assistant checked a few boxes on his

form and held out his hand. "I can take your key downstairs for you so you can be on your way if you'd like. Did you end up deciding to go back to Michigan?"

Perdue pulled the key from his keyring and handed it to Littlejohn. "No, I've got a place here in Jackson where I'm going to stay."

"Found a classmate in town to stay with?" the RA asked as he checked another box on his form. When he looked up, though, Perdue was already ducking into the stairwell.

Perdue had his choice of parking spots close to the cafeteria. He pulled his truck into one in front of the entrance and embarked on one of his many walks around campus. The cafeteria wouldn't open for another two hours, so he took his time. As he passed the physical plant, he heard the whine of a circular saw and ventured closer. He hadn't used his tools since he arrived in Jackson. Maybe, he thought, he could befriend a worker here and ask to use the facilities.

———

"HEY, KID, WHATCHA DOIN'?" asked a slender dark-skinned gentleman in a long-sleeved work shirt. He looked to be in his sixties. "You need somethin'?"

"Oh, no, sir, not exactly."

"Sir? You ain't from around here, are ya?"

"No, sir, I'm from Michigan. Is my accent that bad?"

"Naw. Just ain't many white boys from Miss'ippi gonna call a colored man *sir*. Whatcha need?"

"I heard your saw and... well, I do some wood-working myself, and I just wanted to walk over and see what you're working on."

"Buildin' a bookshelf for a professor's office right now." The colored man grinned, exposing the dozen teeth left in his mouth. "What kind of stuff you make?"

"Mostly porch swings. I paid my way to school by making them and selling them back home."

"Your daddy teach you to do that?"

"No, my dad died when I was two weeks old. A man named Mr. Mitchell taught me how to woodwork. He was going to show me all about carpentry during the summers I was in high school, but he died near the end of my freshman year. I used what he taught me to pay my way from Michigan to here, but I... hey, my name is Herschel Perdue. What's your name?"

"Perdue, huh? My name's Reeves. Willis Reeves. Been workin' here at the college since I gave up drivin' a pulpwood truck 'bout ten years ago. I get to build things and fix stuff, so I like it. Tell me 'bout you, Perdue. You want a cup of cool water?"

Over several Dixie cups of water on a warm December afternoon, Herschel told a colored gentleman he just met the background that Chris Littlejohn hadn't been able to pull from him over several months. Talking to Willis Reeves reminded Perdue of how his younger self had opened up to Mr. Mitchell. Reeves mumbled and nodded from time to time to let Herschel know he was still listening, but he listened without a word.

When his new acquaintance stopped, Reeves said, "That's quite a story you've got there, young fella."

"Not one I would have chosen, that's for sure. I'm

sorry if you didn't want to hear all that. I'm sure neither one of us woke up this morning expecting this conversation."

"For sure, that's true. Folks always told me I was a good listener."

"You are, and I appreciate it more than you know. Mr. Reeves?"

"You're best off to just call me Reeves. Don't let your white classmates—the ones that's from these parts anyhow—don't let 'em hear you callin' a black man *mister*."

"But what if I want to? I thought showing respect to your elders was a big part of southern manners?"

"That's true, that is. Good manners for white young folks to show respect to white old folks and good manners for black young folks to show respect to black old folks. For black young folks to show respect to white old folks is more than good manners; they better show 'em respect lest they want to find themselves strung up in a tree. And white young folks ain't got no obligations to show respect to old black folks. Some of 'em do, but they're the exception."

"Mr. Reeves…"

"Just Reeves."

"All right, Just Reeves, do… uh… do white people here… do they still lynch black people? That part of history is… history, right?"

"Progress comes slow in this part of the country, Perdue. I don't know what it's like where you're from, but 'round here if you're black, you still better play it smart when you're 'round white folks."

"But doesn't that make you feel like a second-class citizen?"

"Now you figgerin' it out. Don't get me wrong, young fella, I like what I do here at the college, but I just say *yes sir* when them professors come down here and tell me to make somethin' for 'em. They don't do it much, but when they want a new bookshelf for their offices, they know I'll make 'em a topnotch one, even if they don't go through my boss to get it."

"That's your specialty, huh? What do you get for a bookcase?" Herschel asked, pointing to a five-shelver that was completed and coated with varnish.

"Sometimes they say *thank you*. Not to mention other ones of 'em show up down here askin' for one for their office. I got five or six ordered right now for when they get back from the school break."

"Wait, so this is not part of your job and they still don't pay you for them? This is good work. One like this has got to be worth thirty or forty dollars."

Reeves grinned. "You like 'em that much? Naw, I pick up extra wood when we finish a job on the campus and bring it back here. I don't mind much. I make enough here to help at home, and I figger the more I keep the professors happy, the better the chance they'll brag on my work to somebody that matters. My wife, she passed three or four years ago, and I live with my daughter now. Her husband is the janitor at one of the grammar schools, and she picks up money ironing clothes for folks, so my paycheck helps them. They got four children, my grandchildren, so I'm blessed to be close to all of 'em. We grow a garden and raise pigs and chickens, so I've got plenty to do here and at home, which is all a lonely old man can ask for. You and me, we're a lot alike, wouldn't you say, young Mr. Perdue?"

"Yes, sir, I suppose so."

"Boy, you better stop it with the *yes sirs.*"

"Sorry." Herschel wasn't sorry. "Uh, Mr. Reeves, I mean, Reeves?"

"Yes, sir?"

"Are you going to be here working during Christmas break?"

"I 'spect so, except for Christmas Eve and Christmas Day."

"Would you teach me to make bookcases like you do? I could bring my own tools and help you."

"Son, I ain't got no money to pay you. I told you, they don't pay me nothin' for these bookcases."

"Oh, I wouldn't want any money from you, just a little mentoring."

"I don't know…"

"I'd bring my own tools since I know a man doesn't like somebody else using his tools."

"You right, but it ain't that so much that as what folks might think if they saw us working together."

"If this is the time you make bookcases every day, don't you imagine the folks working through the holidays will have already gone home?"

"That's true right there. My boss leaves by three o'clock in the afternoon at the very latest. I'm always glad to lock up for him, and he's always glad to let me. I get started on these here 'bout ten minutes after he drives off. He knows about 'em, but what he don't see, he don't have to report. What he knows, though, is if the professors are happy with us, the higher-ups is gonna be happy with us."

"So it's okay if I come after your boss leaves?"

"Well…" Reeves scratched his head.

"Tell you what—I'll bring some wood and teach you how I make my swings. If you know anybody who might want one, I'll split the profit with you."

"You would do that?"

"Sure. I love this stuff."

"You young folks from the north sure is different from the ones 'round these parts."

"Perhaps, but I was an oddball up there, too, so I'm not the best representative of boys from the north."

"Speakin' of that, young fella, you ain't got no place to go up there in Michigan?"

"No, sir—oh, sorry. No, once I aged out of the boys' home, I'm no longer eligible to live there, even for Christmas break. I figured it was time to strike out on my own. I just hadn't counted on the dorms closing down for the break."

"Yeah, it gives us physical plant folks a chance to go in and fix what needs fixin', plus it lets all the folks in charge of the dorms have a good long vacation, I reckon. So you stayin' with a family here in Jackson?"

Herschel hadn't mentioned his accommodations. Perhaps if he could sell a few swings, he could spend more of the break at the Sun-n-Sand and enjoy a healthier diet. "Yeah, staying local. So if I come by here about three-thirty Monday afternoon, you'll be here?"

"I'll be here. Make sure the two-tone blue pickup is

gone—that's my boss's truck. He leaves somewhere between two and two-thirty when the students is on break, so if you want to check by a little earlier, I 'spect you can come on in. Park out back of the building where you see my green truck. Well, Perdue, it's startin' to get dark outside, so I'm gonna call it a day."

"Dark? Oh my goodness, I've got to get up to the cafeteria to eat my supper. Thanks for talking to me, mist—uh, Reeves. I'll see you on Monday afternoon."

Herschel bounded out of the physical plant and up the hill to eat his supper. Three others, all international students, ate alone at various tables, and a couple shared a last meal together before they went their separate ways for a month. Otherwise, the dining hall was a ghost town. Herschel stuffed his pockets full of saltines at the salad bar and then piled his plate high with everything he could fit on his plate. He asked for extra fries to go with his cheeseburger and sat down to devour the meal that he hoped would stave off hunger until the following morning.

When Herschel finished his meal and stuffed a few more saltines in his jacket pocket, he walked out into the chilly evening and moved his truck a block over from the school's north entrance. He carried his rolled up sleeping bag under his left arm and a grocery bag with a change of clothes and a few toiletries in his right. Not wanting to attract attention as a transient, he scanned each intersection before he stepped out to cross each street. When he reached his destination, he peered as far as he could in each direction before stepping over a knee-high decorative fence. When he was under the cover of several large evergreen shrubs, he pulled a flashlight from the back pocket of his jeans to light the way to the treehouse. He flung his sleeping bag toward the narrow opening. It rebounded to him, and he searched for anyone who might have witnessed his misstep. When he saw no one, he tried again, this time with success, and clambered up the wooden steps after it.

The inside of the treehouse was roomy and clean and enclosed except for the entrance and a pair of opposing windows. Hershel hoped to stay warm enough during the mid-December night and quiet enough not to attract any attention. The treehouse was barely visible from the street, even in the wintertime, because of its color, the tall boxwood hedge along the street, and the evergreen shrubs that guarded the path entrance to the property. He set his internal clock to the pre-dawn hours, rolled up his sweatshirt to use as a pillow, and slipped inside his sleeping bag for the night. The floor was hard but free, and the night sounds were peaceful.

Herschel drifted off quickly but awakened in the wee hours of the morning to a distant *thump, thump, thump* that drew closer as he listened. His watch showed 4:14, eight hours after he had dozed off. The noise grew steadily louder. *Thump, thump, thump*. Steady but not regular. Through one tiny opening in the hedge, Herschel discovered the paper boy as the source of his alarm. Perfect. If he delivers at the same time every morning, Herschel would be gone before anybody else was up. After changing clothes and running a comb through his hair, he rolled the rest of his belongings into his sleeping bag and started down the steps. His eyes darted up the lane toward the house, still dark. He slipped over the fence and back toward school, where he enjoyed seeing the morning come alive on a brisk walk around the campus. Back at his truck, he nibbled on some crackers to soothe the beast coming alive in his stomach, though his mouth was dry.

A little after 8:00, he stopped by at a neighborhood diner for a glass of orange juice and a sausage and cheese omelet. A local in a work shirt that read *Harold* gave Herschel directions to the nearest lumber yard. He spent most of the rest of the morning gathering the wood and hardware he would need to assemble his swings. He picked up a thermos at a discount store and filled it from a water fountain in a park near Millsaps. At 2:00, he parked across the street from the physical plant, looking for a two-tone blue truck to pull out of the parking lot. It didn't appear by 2:30, or by 3:00, or by 3:30. At 4:00, Herschel pulled his truck around the physical plant building, but found the area in the back where the employees parked deserted. Then it occurred to him that this was Saturday, and he was two days early.

Scrounging through the garbage container outside the back door of the building produced a piece of black plastic large enough to cover the lumber in the back of Perdue's truck. He piddled the rest of the afternoon and ate an early supper at Shoney's, pocketing another handful of crackers to eat at his new home away from the dorm. Shortly after dark, after scrubbing his face and neck in the restroom at the restaurant, he slipped back into the treehouse. This time, he swapped out a change of clothes for his thermos and business textbook. Clean clothes could wait until he returned to his truck in the early morning hours.

The street was empty at seven o'clock when Herschel mounted the steps to the treehouse. The main house was still dark, and he wondered if anyone was home. As far as he had ever been able to tell from his neighborhood walks, only the couple in their sixties occupied the house. Apparently, they did all of their own landscaping since he had never seen evidence of any other family or even a housekeeper. Emboldened by the further isolation of his dwelling, he tucked himself into the corner farthest from the treehouse's opening and flipped on his flashlight to re-read his business textbook.

Herschel's academic counselor had informed him that a high percentage of college students changed their majors during their college careers. He encouraged him to stay open to other options during his freshman year. However, Herschel's desire to study business had only strengthened during his first semester. General business was the only class from his major on his first term schedule, but he had already read the textbook twice. It was his easiest A in a semester filled with them. With no further obligations to the class, he opened the book to re-read the section on management. It was bookmarked with a sheet of yellow paper labeled "One Day When I Run My Own Business." Beneath the heading, Herschel had jotted ideas about how he planned to manage finances, resources, and people when he attached his name to a business.

He turned his attention to one of his most recent notes: "Owners get so caught up in the day-to-day operations during their company's early growth that they don't empower employees to handle that growth. I'm going to figure out how to see my employees' potential to impact the company early in their careers and guide them to maximize it." *Sounds like an idealistic college student wrote that. How will I make that happen? The book doesn't give much direction on people skills. Maybe that comes later in the higher level courses.* Herschel had his doubts, though, because he had noticed that none of the business classes taught sales. Another of the notes on his page said, "Sales seems to be so much about pressuring a customer to buy something he doesn't need. What if I could flip that to produce something the customer already wants but can't get? That would seem to ease frustration for the customer, and wouldn't that make him more loyal?" *Perhaps the real world will reveal the academic silliness of such an idea,* he now thought, *but it's worth a shot.* He drifted off to sleep an hour later with visions of his future business in his head, and the light from his flashlight still sucking the life out of its batteries.

10

BOOM!

A peel of thunder awakened Hershel around five o'clock. A check through the narrow opening down the street revealed he had slept through the paper boy's delivery. Marking the time between the thunder and lightning, he judged he had just five minutes to reach the safety of his truck. The untarnished floor of the tree-house suggested he would stay dry there, but he didn't want to be trapped in the tree. The chances of anyone seeing him there during a thunderstorm were minuscule, but what if he needed to go to the bathroom... like now. *Four minutes.* He slid down the ladder with little concern for onlookers in the dark, stormy morning hours. He sprinted the three-quarters of a mile to his truck, fumbled with his keys as the first drops fell, and threw himself across the seat about the time the bottom fell out of the sky.

Hershel slowed his breathing and stretched out to sleep away the rest of the early morning hours. The rain was soothing, though the lightning was too close for his comfort. He awoke with a start an hour later. *My things are still in the treehouse!*

While concerned about his belongings, Hershel carried out his plan for Sunday before trying to retrieve them. He figured the very early morning hours of Sunday morning were the best opportunity he would have to bathe himself in the school fountain with no gawkers. A brisk wind followed the storms, so he would make quick work of it. He parked to the side of the administration building and strolled as casually as he could around front—as casually as the only student on campus carrying a towel and a bar of soap could. He peeked in every direction before he sprang from the bushes in front of the building for a three-minute bath, wearing just his boxers. When he slipped out of his converted bathtub, he threw the towel around his shoulders and sprinted for the bushes. There, he toweled off and adorned a clean set of clothes as the security guard walked up the sidewalk near him unaware. Once he arrived at his truck, he applied deodorant and combed his hair to finish transforming from vagabond back to college student. His still-elevated heart rate decided that his next dip in the fountain would come under the cover of darkness.

Now for his belongings, still trapped in the tree-house. If his neighbors were like most people in the South, they would attend one of the downtown churches during the 11:00 hour, giving him a window of opportunity he wouldn't have on any other day. He couldn't be so careless again, he admonished himself. Herschel walked the neighborhood opposite his usual route, passing the main house to his left and approaching the treehouse in the back after checking the houses and yards on that street for activity. He hustled up the edge of the grass lane, climbed the ladder to scoop up his things, and carried them back to the street. He still saw no movement, so he stepped over the fence and made his way back to his truck. *Whew, made it! I MUST be more careful. Another day like today, and I'll get busted for trespassing.*

Herschel's body heat eventually returned to normal from his outdoor bath. He nibbled on his stash of saltines until the lunch crowd at the restaurants dwindled before trekking to the Elite on Capitol Street, a popular restaurant in a brick building from another era. Some parts of the culture of the South were still foreign to him, but he had warmed to southern cuisine with little problem. He enjoyed a plate of fried chicken and mashed potatoes with gravy, along with the Elite's famous yeast rolls. Two more rolls made their way into his jacket pocket for later.

After a day of near misses trying to establish his Christmas break routine, Herschel mapped out a schedule for the rest of the break. He would risk staying in the treehouse until the week of Christmas, unless he spotted guests in the main house. His modified budget after his trip to the lumber yard allowed a week at the

Sun-n-Sand, especially if he sold a few swings in the coming week. He figured to check in every third or fourth day anyway in order to shower and shave. His face itched with a few days' growth of facial hair, but he would just have to deal with that. He was clean, which was sufficient for today. What he missed was social interaction. Two o'clock Monday afternoon couldn't arrive soon enough.

HERSHEL PARKED his truck around the corner from the Millsaps physical plant by 1:45 Monday afternoon. Right at two o'clock, the two-tone blue truck turned the corner. Five minutes later, Herschel pulled up next to Willis Reeves's truck. Reeves was working on the same bookcase from Friday when Herschel stepped in the shop carrying his tool bag.

"Hey, Mr. Reeves!"

Reeves jumped. "Geez, Perdue, don't be sneaking up on an old black man! And I done told you, it's just *Reeves*. Leave the *mister* up north. Kinda surprised to see you back today."

"Want to hear something funny? I was here Saturday. I lost track of the days."

"Don't have no bell telling you when to stand up and when to move, do ya?"

"A bell?"

"When you work at a school but ain't no student or professor or nothing, you notice things those folks don't. Like bells. Bell rings, all you folks get up and start movin' somewheres. Ain't nobody got to tell you what to do 'cause the bells done got y'all conditioned to do it. Me, I be workin' in one of the classroom buildings and a bell rings, I keep doin' what I was doin'. Bell don't mean nothin' to me, except for more young folks steppin' around me whilst I do my work."

"Never thought about it like that."

"Course you haven't 'cause you a rat in the race."

"I know what you mean about noticing things other folks don't, though, living all these years as an orphan."

"I expect you have, at that. You ready to get started?"

"Chomping at the bit."

"You know what that means, do ya?"

"Sort of. I hear people down here say it when they're looking forward to something."

Reeves chuckled. "That's it, that's it. Sounds like you've taken to southern talk like a duck to water."

"A duck to water?"

"Something comes second nature to you."

The two worked together mostly in silence, other than an occasional instruction to cut a board or nail it in place. Reeves grunted his approval each time Herschel completed a new task. After piecing together a bookcase, he said, "Perdue, you do good work for a boy your age."

"Thank you, sir."

"Now if I could just break you from callin' me *sir* and *mister*, we would work all right together."

"Sorry—habit."

"Ain't a terrible habit, no, sir. You keep callin' your

white professors *sir* and *mister* here and your bosses
when you get out..."

"I'm not planning to have a boss, ever. I want to start
a business as soon as I finish my degree, or before."

"Always gonna have somebody to answer to,
Perdue, whether it's the boss man or the tax man or the
policeman."

"Oh, I know that. But as I look at people who run
their own businesses—how they treat their customers
and how they treat their own employees—and I believe
I can improve on that. I think if I can put other people
ahead of myself, I can still make a profit while I'm, you
know, building them up."

"Mm-hmm." Reeves wrestled with his own thoughts
while sanding a one-by-twelve plank to be used for a
shelf on the new bookcase he had just started. "That's
usin' the golden rule, and folks don't do that too much
in they businesses. 'Specially with black folks—always
thinkin' you tryin' to cheat 'em when they's the ones
tryin' to cheat you. You gonna treat niggers the same
way you treat white folks, Perdue?"

"Why wouldn't I?"

"Why wouldn't you. Maybe we'll talk about this
again when you get outta school, and we see how much
of the South rubs off on your white behind."

"I'm not a racist, Mr. Reeves."

"Not yet, you ain't. You been here how long, five
months?"

"About."

"Mm-hmm."

"You don't like white people, do you, Mr. Reeves?"

Reeves never looked up. "Ain't that I don't like 'em, just don't trust 'em. They'll say one thing to your face and then twist the knife in your back."

"Not all of us."

"Mm-hmm."

Herschel stopped sanding and turned to face Willis Reeves. "Reeves, can I tell you something?"

"I reckon."

"Do you remember me telling you about Mr. Mitchell?"

"Mitchell—the man who taught you how to build things?"

"He was more than a master carpenter. He was a mentor to me, more of a father figure than I've had before or since."

"Mm-hmm." Reeves continued to slide his long manual sander across the wood.

"And he was a black man."

Reeves stopped. "No kiddin'?"

"No kidding. I didn't know until later that the rest of the boys in the home where I lived didn't want to learn from him because he was black. I think they were more scared than prejudiced, but still... they missed out, but their loss was my gain. If the rest of the boys had stuck with carpentry lessons, Mr. Mitchell would have been more of a teacher to us than a personal mentor to me. My point, Mr. Reeves, is that if respect had a skin color, my experience says to respect yours perhaps even more than mine. If that's a deal killer for you, I'm sorry, but I think I could learn a lot from you."

Reeves laid his sander on the table in front of him

and locked eyes with the peculiar white student who had barged into his life uninvited. "I 'spect there's a lot we could learn from each other, Perdue." His eyes were moist when he said it. He claimed sawdust in his eyes and rubbed them hard. "You said you could teach me how to make a porch swing."

"I imagine you would make a fine porch swing on your own, but I'll be glad to show you how Mr. Mitchell taught me. I have the wood in the bed of my truck. Want to help me bring it in? I have enough to make four swings. It won't take long with two of us working on them."

As the pair walked side by side to Herschel's truck, Reeves asked, "Perdue, you know one name white folks has for niggers?"

"I don't care for that word, but I thought that was it."

"Naw, they got all sorts of names for us—*apes, coons, picaninnies, bluegums, sambos.* Another one of 'em is *porch monkeys.*"

"Why do they call you that?"

"Well, they call us *monkeys* because we're black. I reckon they call us *porch monkeys* 'cause that's where we congregate with our families and neighbors. Most of our porches is small 'cause our houses is small, so I reckon we kind of spill out of 'em. It's hot around here most of the year, too blamed hot to sit inside a house that ain't air conditioned. We spend a lot of time on the porch or under a big shade tree, if we got one. The way I figure it, if they's gonna drive by and call me a porch monkey, I might as well be porch monkeyin' in a decent swing. Let's get started."

———

By the time the sun had set, Perdue and Reeves had completed all four porch swings. Herschel told his new business partner that he planned to hawk the swings from the back of his truck in downtown Jackson the following day. Reeves directed him toward a prime spot where traffic would be heavy in the morning and the evening.

As they carried the fourth swing out, Herschel said, "This one's for you, Mr. Reeves."

"Naw, young fella, I can't be takin' it. That's your college money."

"I want you to have it. You see how quickly we can make them, so I'll have plenty to sell. It means a lot that you've given me a chance to work and to learn from you. Please, take it."

"I ain't ever had white folks give me much of nothing but a hard time." Sawdust returned to his eyes, though he had put his equipment away thirty minutes earlier. "Thank you, Perdue," he whispered.

Filthy and sweaty from his afternoon's work, Hershel enjoyed a lengthy dip in the school fountain before dining on a sackful of Krystal burgers back at the treehouse. The next morning, he awoke to the sound of Tuesday issues of *The Clarion Ledger* plopping on the driveways up the street. Refreshed and motivated for his day's work, he bounded down the ladder with all of his belongings accounted for this time. He had just stepped over the decorative metal fence when headlights from down the street lit his path. He scampered around the corner onto the dark adjoining street and strolled to his truck, where a Jackson police officer stood waiting for him.

11

"Hi, officer, is there a problem?"

"This your truck?"

Herschel recognized that the policeman was a no-nonsense type. "Yes, sir."

"Neighbors been complaining that it doesn't belong here."

"Is it illegal to park here?"

"Not illegal, just irregular. Makes me wonder what you're up to."

"I'm not up to anything. I'm a Millsaps student, first year, and I've been staying with a friend over the break."

"Y'aint from around here, are ya?"

"No, sir, originally from Michigan."

"Yankee, huh?"

"Yes, sir, I suppose so, but I enjoy it here so far."

"Well, that's good, I guess. Just be careful about

bringing in any outside ways. Folks don't take kindly to a lot of change and fancy ideas around here."

"Yes, sir."

"What's with the sleeping bag? And tell me—what is a college student doing awake this time of the morning? I thought you boys slept until noon on days you didn't have school."

"Oh, uh, my friend and I were studying. I took a sleeping bag in case we slept, but we didn't."

"So ya'll were pulling an all-nighter during Christmas break? Y'all been doin' any drinkin', Mr. Perdue?"

Herschel reached for his textbook, which was rolled up in his sleeping bags.

"Whoa, there, cap'n. Whatcha reachin' for?"

He produced his textbook. "Just this."

"Okay, but you don't need to be making any sudden movements like that, you hear?"

"Yes, sir. I'm sorry."

"So what's this?"

"Business textbook. My friend and I have been making notes on types of businesses we'd like to start when we graduate."

Herschel had successfully lost the officer's interest, which now turned to the bed of his truck. "What's back here under the plastic?"

"Porch swings. I've been making them since I was in ninth grade. I made a few yesterday, hoping to sell them and make a little money for school."

"Oh, yeah? Mind if I look?" His interest seemed genuine, especially after Herschel removed his makeshift tarpaulin. "Say, these are pretty good," the police officer said, running his hand along the lines. "How much you asking for them?"

"Forty dollars."

"Where are you selling them?"

Herschel laughed nervously. "Out of the back of my truck, I hope."

"Mm-hmm." He offered a spot to park to sell the swings, the same one Mr. Reeves had suggested, then changed direction. "I need to check your license."

Hershel's heart jumped back into his throat. He couldn't determine why this discussion had tarried so long. If he wasn't parked in an illegal spot, and he had answered the other questions honestly—well, at least logically—then why was he still on trial? He handed over the license.

"Perdue, huh?" the officer asked, one eye upturned as his gaze fixed on Herschel's face.

"Yes, sir, Herschel Perdue."

"Mr. Perdue, I'm Officer Larry Gaines. Nice to meet you. Do me a couple of favors, will ya."

"Yes, sir."

"You stay at this friend's house again, park at his house instead of out here on the street."

"Yes, sir."

"And put my name on one of those swings of yours. My shift ends at eight, and I'll come by the spot I mentioned and pay you for it."

"Yes, sir, I'll be glad to."

"All right, get moving."

"Yes, sir, and thank you. I'll see you a little after eight."

David laughed at Perdue's story. "Were you scared?"

"You better believe I was scared. It was four-thirty in the morning, just me and a cop awake on this neighborhood street, college kid from the North walking around carrying a sleeping bag. It was beneficial for me to have my textbook with me with my notes in it. That line about staying at a friend's house was the only lie I told, and I had enough proof with my textbook to sufficiently bore him to death with that line of questioning."

"Did he show up to buy his swing?"

"Sure did. I sold the other two to his captain and another officer the next day."

"That was pretty good money for a day's work for a college student then, wasn't it?"

"Yeah, but remember, I needed to repay myself for the materials it took to build them, and I had promised Willis Reeves half the profit for letting me use the shop at school to make them. Plus, I had more materials to buy, hoping the rest of the swings I built would sell that quickly."

"I'll bet you wish you hadn't been so quick to offer him half."

"No regrets at all. I got lonesome living on my own like that. Three or four hours' worth of conversation with a real live human being, especially one as interesting as Mr. Reeves, was worth it. What little I profit I had left I used to check into the Sun-n-Sand for the rest of the week. I worked in the afternoons and had a legal place to go clean up afterward without freezing myself to death."

"And all the bologna and crackers you could eat?"

"Yeah, there was that, but my capacity for bologna and crackers waned as the days went by. I also needed to figure out what I was going to do with the rest of my break. Before Christmas, I ended up selling five more swings. I stayed at the Sun-n-Sand through Christmas, but I had to come up with a plan to get back to 'my' treehouse before I spent everything I made on showers and bologna and crackers. I knew Officer Gaines would recognize my truck if he was patrolling the neighborhood, and so would other officers on his shift who had come by to look at my swings. I decided to leave my truck on campus because there were several stray vehicles in the parking lots from students who had flown somewhere for the break.

"It was a good two-mile hike from school to the treehouse, which I didn't mind at all unless it was raining. I decided to leave my sleeping bag at the treehouse and leave the rest of my stuff like clothes and toiletries in my truck. I would keep my book with me in case I got stopped again since I really was studying and because that excuse had worked so well with Officer Gaines. One risk I couldn't get around was bathing in the fountain at night. If the weather got too bad, I checked into the motel."

"You had it all figured out, didn't you?"

Perdue chuckled. "Well, I thought I did."

"How did Mr. Reeves react when you paid him his share?"

"Over the moon. He figured I would finagle the numbers, you know, cheat him somehow. But I played it straight and gave him his full share."

"Plus the swing."

"Plus the swing. It was all worth it for me, though, because, one, I had a place to make my swings and, two, I had someone to talk to during those long, lonely days. I don't think I understood the reality of living on my own. Before I left for school, I determined to make it work somehow, and I knew I would be a stronger person on the other side of it. However, I didn't quite bargain on sneaking baths from the school fountain under the cover of darkness." Perdue threw his head back a laughed at the vision of his younger self, drawing stares from others near them in the dining hall. "Oh, what a funny sight I must have been. Grab us another dessert, would you? They're probably going to ask for our table here pretty soon if we look like we're finished."

DAVID TOOK plates of pecan and sweet potato pie from the dessert table and brought them back to the corner table where Perdue was still smiling about his vagabond days. "Pecan or sweet potato—your choice. I'm fine with whichever one you don't want. I'll eat anything sweet."

Perdue chose pecan. "Look, David, you've been

patient with an old man, so I won't keep you much longer. You did a good job on my broken pane for somebody who doesn't do that kind of thing for a living. As far as my story goes, I'll share one more part of my college story over dessert and let you be on your way."

"Oh, no, sir, you're not getting rid of me that easily. You've got me hooked and unless you've got other plans today and you're kicking me out, I'm sticking around for all of it."

Perdue's smile spoke volumes, though his eyes hinted that the loneliness that he spoke of from his college days had returned, even in this place where people surrounded him day and night. "Okay, then. I'll finish this one up and go on to the next chapter in the library. That's where I spend most of my days, working on my book and reading. People have learned to leave me alone there."

"I would have figured with the loneliness you've felt in the past, you would want the company."

"Company like this," he said, motioning back and forth between himself and David, "I enjoy. I can engage in meaningful conversation all day long. But bingo games, group exercise, '60's singalongs, pudding tastings, and such don't interest me."

"Pudding tastings?"

"A bit of hyperbole, perhaps, but you get the point."

David nodded, wiped his mouth after finishing his pie, and sat back in his chair so Perdue could continue with his story.

"I'M HERE, MR. REEVES!"

"Dadgummit, don't be scarin' an old black man sneakin' up behind him like that. You'll get yourself shot, boy."

"I wasn't sneaking up on you. I just…"

"I reckon it seems like sneakin' to an old man who's been using power tools for too long without protectin' his ears."

"Sorry."

"It's all right. You need to make more swings today?"

"Nah, I have two left, and tomorrow's Christmas Eve. I'd rather sell them and not have to keep them in the back of my truck."

"I'ma take the rest of the week off, so don't be comin' 'round here expectin' to find me. I'll be spendin' time with that grandbaby o' mine swingin' in our new porch swing."

The holidays had always seemed lonely to Herschel, especially after he reached junior high school and felt the gravity of being a foster kid. Then, he was still a couple of years away from the boys' home, where they celebrated holidays more like what he considered a normal family might. He felt like a spectator with the foster families at Christmas, watching them exchange gifts as if he wasn't in the room. Oh, there was usually one gift under the tree for him, a second-hand shirt or a toy with which the older kids no longer played. Several times, he had overheard a foster parent say that he should be grateful to have a roof over his head and food to eat.

"I wasn't that needy. I was grateful." The blank stare on Reeves's face when he said it informed Hershel that the thoughts in his head had leaked out. Sheepishly, he backed up and filled in the sizable conversation gap.

"Where you stayin' for Christmas, Perdue?"

"At the S—" Oops, almost let it slip. "At my friend's house."

"What's this friend's name?"

"Uh, S—Sonny Sandifer." He laughed internally at his quick creation, being careful that his thoughts stayed private this time.

"You stayin' with this Sonny Sandifer the entire break?"

"Just parts of it. I've been moving around some."

"Mm-hmm. All right, Perdue, we got to put the finishin' touches on this here bookcase, and then we gonna call it a day."

"When are you coming back to work?"

"You that eager to get back to it, are ya? You ain't gonna have no market for them swings, you know, except for a day or two after Christmas when people got money burnin' a hole in they pocket."

Herschel wished he had considered that his well was about to run dry. He had made a deal with himself to limit his nights at "Sonny Sandifer's" to what his profits from his swings would afford. With no further sales, he had enough money in his pocket to stay through the day after Christmas and on weekends and to eat two or three meals a day. He would sure miss the warm showers and the indoor plumbing, but he would not miss bologna and crackers. In a strange sort of way, he missed the adventure of living in the treehouse. He seemed to think better there, too, maybe because his nerves were a little more on edge, but it's where his business plan was coming together.

At four o'clock, when Reeves was ready to call it a day, Herschel parked at the Sun-n-Sand, smirking when he passed the front desk. In his mind, he said *Evening, Sonny*, to the clerk. After a quick shower and a bologna and cracker sandwich, he took a walk with just his tape measure, pencil, and notepad to keep him company. In the fading light of the early winter day, he clambered up his treehouse and jotted down the measurements. *I'm going to build this treehouse one day.*

Back at the Sun-n-Sand later, the clerk called him over. "Perdue, right?"

"That's me."

"Someone left a package for you." He reached under the counter and produced a shoebox-sized package, wrapped with red paper with Merry Christmas printed on the side. Herschel thanked the clerk and rushed to his room to tear into what would be his only Christmas gift of 1971. He tore through the wrapping, opening a box full of homemade cookies and other goodies, accompanied by a handwritten note: *Thought you might like these to get the taste of bologna out of your mouth. P.S.: Much better choice on your parking spot.* Herschel considered how thoughtful it was for Officer Gaines to bring him a gift and how spooky it was that the policeman knew where he was staying. He dismissed it as the cost of driving a bright yellow truck that still bore a Michigan tag. He would change the tag soon enough, but he couldn't do much about the color.

———

HERSCHEL SOLD the last two porch swings early on Christmas Eve to a pair of husbands thankful to find such thoughtful gifts for their wives so close to Christmas. The Sun-n-Sand was practically empty, with only Herschel and three families in town to visit with relatives at arm's length. Some Pepperidge Farm summer sausage and crackers from his gift basket were a festive improvement over the usual lunch of bologna and crackers. He chose the Mayflower Cafe, a downtown Jackson staple about which he had heard rave reviews from all the locals, for his big Christmas meal. It was too expensive for his budget, but this was Christmas Eve and the closest he would come to celebrating the holiday with other people. He imagined having the Sun-n-Sand to himself for most of the following day.

The restaurant was crowded for Christmas Eve, he thought, but it was also a Friday night. He felt a little guilty taking a table for two when others were waiting, but his waitress put him at ease. She didn't ask nosy questions, acting like it was the most normal thing in the world for a teenager to be eating out alone in downtown Jackson on Christmas Eve. She introduced herself as Susan. She was about his age, and Herschel liked her right away.

"What can I get you to drink?"

"Tea."

"Sweet tea?" she drawled the Southern nectar.

Hershel chuckled. "I'm still transitioning to the fully loaded stuff. Could you make mine half sweet and half unsweet?"

"Sure, I can do that. Where are you from?"

"Michigan."

"Here for school?"

"Yeah, I just finished my first semester at Millsaps."

"Oh, smart guy."

"I work hard. My name is Perdue—Herschel Perdue. Do you have a last name, Susan?"

"Susan Taylor. What brought you to Mississippi to go to school, Herschel?"

"I wanted to study business, and I applied to schools all over the country. I couldn't afford to pay for college with my savings, so it came down to which top-notch school was going to offer me the most scholarship money, and in the end, that's how I chose Millsaps."

"That's neat. You must have made excellent grades in high school to even get into Millsaps, much less get that much scholarship money."

"Good grades, but not great. I think it was more of my story and my experience starting a business in ninth grade that convinced the scholarship committee to give me a chance."

"Sound like an interesting story. I'd love to hear it sometime. Listen, I gotta get back to work. I'll be right back with that half-and-half tea. Which one do you want on top?"

"Huh?"

Susan laughed. "Little tip: If you sip the tea straight

from the glass like most southerners do, the tea is going to taste like whatever is on top. If the sweet is on top, it's almost the same as drinking sweet tea; if the unsweet is on top, it's like drinking unsweet." She inched closer, covering half of her face with her order pad and added, "Most people down South would say that if the unsweet is on top, it tastes like… something else."

"Then give it to me with the sweet on top. And thanks for the tip, Susan Taylor."

Walking away, she said over her shoulder, "One good tip deserves another, right?"

Oh, she's good, Herschel thought. He imagined a wink accompanying her comeback. With no resistance, he followed her suggestion of the redfish and fries with comeback sauce. His meal did not disappoint. During her comings and goings from his table, he discovered she was a freshman at Hinds Junior College in Raymond. She was waiting tables during the break in order to save money toward attending the University of Southern Mississippi, where she planned to pursue a degree in elementary education. It was a career that seemed to fit her.

When the time came for the inevitable question of whether he had saved room for dessert, he would have answered in the affirmative to anything she suggested. The homemade lemon icebox pie, though, stood on its own merits. With no further reason to extend his stay, he pulled enough cash out of his wallet to pay his bill and dove back in for a more generous tip than he had ever given. He gave it to his new favorite server and told her to keep the change.

"Are you sure?" she asked. "It's my biggest tip of the night."

Herschel smiled at that. "Like you said, one good tip deserves another."

"Well, thank you, Hershel."

"You're welcome, Susan. You know, I'm just a broke college student who can't afford to eat at the Mayflower except on special occasions, but I would like to see you again." It was his first meaningful advance toward a girl, and it came across less awkwardly than he would have expected. He had been rehearsing it in his mind for the last thirty minutes. From this point on, though, he was in uncharted water.

"Tell you what. You want to see me again, you can find me on Sunday mornings with my family at First Baptist Church. We go to the 11:00 service most weeks, but we'll be attending the 8:00 service tomorrow and then going to my uncle and aunt's house down in Plain. If you need directions to First Baptist, anybody can tell you."

"That's the huge church downtown?"

"Yes, but it's not so big once you meet some people."

"I have watched your church on TV before."

"Not the same as being there live. No pressure, just telling you where I'll be if you want to see me again. It was nice to meet you, Hershel." With that, she spun and walked back to the kitchen. Hershel's mind caught her light brown hair in mid-spin, where it would stay frozen in his mind as he walked the streets of Jackson on a meandering route back to the Sun-n-Sand.

Used to early morning hours, Herschel rose at 4:45 to

shower, shave, and iron the only shirt he deemed appropriate for church. Though he hadn't worn it since school was out for the semester, he had washed it anyway, along with the rest of his clothes, at the laundromat down the street from the Sun-n-Sand. He thought he must be quite the pitiful sight, doing laundry on Christmas Eve night. However, if they could have seen inside his head, they would have seen a motivation unlike Hershel had ever felt before.

12

With so much time to kill before church, Herschel pulled the Gideon Bible from the nightstand drawer. He had never read it before, but he had memorized John 3:16 during a Vacation Bible School at the boys' home. He flipped through the book until he found the Gospel of John and began reading. The reading from the King James Version was difficult at first. It spoke of the Word as if it was a person. When he reached chapter two and read about the miracles of Jesus and some things He said about Himself, his interest piqued. The next thing he knew, he was reading, "It is finished," though the book wasn't quite finished. It caused him to look at the bedside clock, which read 7:55. "Oh, no!" he screamed into his empty room. Scrambling to brush his teeth and knot his only tie the best he knew how, he rushed out the door, darting back in to grab the Gideon's Bible since he didn't own one.

An usher directed him toward toward an empty spot

in the back of the balcony of an otherwise packed auditorium at 8:15. The congregation sang Christmas carols
that sounded somewhat familiar. He moved his lips as
though singing along, meanwhile scanning the room,
upstairs and as much of downstairs as he could see from
his eighth-row perch on the extreme right side of the
balcony. His search for a particular head of light brown
hair proved to be in vain, as most of the young females
at First Baptist shared Susan's hair color. When the
singing was over and the music leader invited everyone
to sit, Herschel scanned the room once more, with no
success. He gave up hope of finding Susan and settled
into the pastor's message. He didn't remember reading
this retelling of the Christmas story in the Gospel of
John earlier that morning.

Herschel panicked near the end of the service when
he calculated the distance between his seat and the
nearest exit. He didn't want to give Susan any chance of
slipping away before he could make his way through
the crowd to find her. After the last prayer, the pastor
wished the members and their guests a Merry
Christmas and segued into announcements about
upcoming events at the church. Herschel slipped out of
his pew and made his way toward the exit, where an
usher blocked the exit to the balcony stairs. He mouthed
"bathroom" and the usher stepped aside and pointed
downstairs. Rushing by him, Herschel reached the
bottom of the stairs as the doors of the main auditorium
burst open, and the lobby flooded with people.

With less than twenty seconds before the crowd from
the balcony forced him from his perch on the fifth step,

he searched frantically for Susan among the burgeoning crowd. When the first congregants from the balcony descended to where he stood, he gave up and joined them in stepping down to the main floor. Dejected, he made his way toward the nearest of several main exits.

"Herschel?"

Turning, he spotted Susan behind the stairwell from which he had come. "Oh, hi."

"Susan, from the Mayflower?"

"I remember you." *I didn't remember your being as beautiful as you are in your white dress and red coat, but I could never forget you.*

"Well, I wondered if you would come. I looked for you before the service, but I didn't see you. Where were you sitting?"

"Up in the balcony. I got here late. Sorry."

She smiled. "Easy to sleep in on a Saturday morning, huh?"

Herschel didn't respond at first, captivated by her smile. "Oh, right, well, no." *Get your stuff together, man.* "Actually, I was up quite early this morning. I read this for the first time." He held up the black Gideon's Bible.

"Here, let me see," she said, reaching for his Bible.

Herschel flinched as he faced the dilemma of admitting that he was staying in a hotel or lying about stealing a Bible from a hotel. *Well done, dummy.* Susan gave the Bible a once-over and handed it back. "What were you reading?"

"What?"

"Yeah, what were you reading this morning from the Bible?"

"Oh, uh, the book of John?"

"Are you asking me or telling me?"

Her smile was disarming, so he relaxed a little. His inner voice told him to quit pretending to be something he was not. After all, they had a pleasant conversation just fifteen hours earlier when he made no presumptions. Funny, his inner voice resembled Willis Reeves's drawl. He realized he was standing in another awkward silence. "Sorry, I was telling you. I couldn't sleep this morning, so I got up and decided I would read the Bible for a while before church. I don't have much experience in that, but I remember being taught John 3:16 somewhere along the way, so I just started there. Next thing I knew, the time had passed for me to leave for church."

"That's kind of cool. Not that you were late, that you got so caught up reading the Bible. How far did you read?"

"The whole thing."

"The entire book of John?"

"Yeah, why?"

"Oh, I don't know. I guess growing up in Sunday school, I'm used to reading a chapter a week, not a complete book of the Bible in one morning."

"Sorry, I didn't know how it worked."

Susan's smile dissipated as she scolded herself. "No, there's no set way to study the Bible, just what I'm used to. I think it's cool that you read the whole thing, kinda different, but in a good way. Did you understand what you read?"

"I understood some, I guess, but I came away with many more questions than answers."

Susan opened her mouth to respond, but turned away when she heard someone calling her name. "Sorry, that's my parents, so I have to go. Like I told you last night, we're going to my uncle's house today to celebrate Christmas with them. I wish I could talk longer."

"Sorry, I don't want to keep you."

"Stop apologizing," she said, swatting his arm. "Maybe we can talk again sometime?"

"Sure, perhaps back here next week?"

"Yes, but on Sunday next week and late service."

"Okay, I'll plan on being here."

Susan walked away, but then turned back. "Get here early enough and you can sit with me and my parents." She pointed toward the right side of the auditorium. "We sit right over there, about halfway toward the front. Maybe afterward, you can eat lunch with us and ask some of your questions?"

"Are you asking me or telling me?" *There you go, boy.*

"That is completely up to you," she countered. With that, she twirled in the opposite direction and walked away, her hair spinning as he had remembered it from the night before at the Mayflower.

DAVID GRINNED and reached for Perdue's dessert plate. "And did you see her again? I'm guessing you did if you still remember it after all these years."

"*All these years.* Watch it with the old jokes, young fella."

"Sorry, I didn't mean it like that."

"Just messing with you. And to answer your question, yes, I saw her again, the next Sunday and most of the rest of the Sundays of her life. I moved to south Mississippi the day I graduated from Millsaps a semester early, and we married on Christmas Eve in 1974. She did her practice teaching the next semester while I started my first actual business. Susan taught for ten years before I hired her away to work for me."

"What… happened?"

"To Susan? Well, we're getting a little ahead of ourselves. If you're going to stay the course and hear my entire life story, then we're going to have to go back to Millsaps for an important piece of the puzzle. What do you say you put those dishes away, and I'll show you to my library?"

"Are you asking me or telling me?"

"You've been paying attention. I like you, David Gull." Perdue led the way to the library, which was as empty as he had expected.

WITH SUSAN out of town and the temperatures moderate, Herschel moved back to the treehouse for a few days. So he didn't show up to First Baptist again wearing his one set of church clothes, he spent some of his Sun-n-Sand budget on dress clothes for the following Sunday. He didn't feel right about swiping the Gideon Bible from the motel, so he bought one of his own from a thrift store. He filled his plentiful spare time reading it by flashlight at night and at various outdoor spots around campus when the ever-changing mid-Mississippi weather allowed.

Herschel returned to the Sun-n-Sand after six uneventful days in the treehouse. His work with Reeves had produced two more swings and a pair of bookcases, one of which was his only sale of the week. He told Reeves about Susan and about his sudden interest in the Bible and about God, but his living arrangement remained a secret. However, he could have sworn he saw Reeves's truck tailing him one day when he left the campus to drive around for a while before parking in the lot nearest his temporary lodging. With no sign of anyone near the treehouse during any of the times he had stayed there, Hershel continued to leave his sleeping bag there. Sometimes, he slept after sunrise and sneaked away after most of the neighbors had left for work, though he risked being spotted by a housewife. His head was swimming with ideas about future business ventures, about a relationship with God, and about Susan. The risk of detection barely dented his thoughts.

SUNDAY MORNING FOUND Hershel at the Sun-n-Sand, awake early and reading his new Bible but checking the clock more regularly than he had the week before. By 10:30, he dressed in his new duds and found his way to First Baptist to wait for Susan in the lobby. She arrived with her parents, dressed smartly in a navy blue dress with white lace around the collar. The nervousness that had evaporated while he was talking to her a week ago crept in again when she introduced him to her parents as her friend. They seemed nice enough, though, and invited him to sit with them for the service. They said nothing of lunch afterward, and neither did Susan, but he enjoyed sitting next to her and talking to her for a few minutes afterward while her parents chatted with friends.

After his hopes for lunch with Susan were dashed, Herschel checked out of the Sun-n-Sand—a late checkout that was a perk for their regulars—since he couldn't bear bologna and crackers. Instead, he sat alone in a cafe, savoring fried chicken and mashed potatoes with gravy while reading through Paul's letter to the Galatians. His reading was casual until he reached chapter four, where verses four to seven jumped off the page at him:

> But when the fulness of the time was come,
>   God sent forth his Son, made of a woman,
>   made under the law,
> To redeem them that were under the law, that
>   we might receive the adoption of sons.
> And because ye are sons, God hath sent forth
>   the Spirit of his Son into your hearts,
>   crying, Abba, Father.
> Wherefore thou art no more a servant, but a
>   son; and if a son, then an heir of God
>   through Christ.

He read it again and then again, churning the implications of adoption to God. All these years, he had placed the hopes of being adopted into the farthest recesses of his mind, content with Ms. Peggy's kindness, Mr. Mitchell's brief mentorship, and now Mr. Reeves's friendship as his loftiest hope. That this God of the universe would send his Son so He could adopt Herschel Perdue into his family was breathtaking. He asked for a doggy bag for the chicken and roll left on his plate, paid his bill, and made for the treehouse to investigate further. By the following Sunday, he was ready to walk down the aisle to give his life to Jesus, since that was the only way he had seen it done.

Susan admitted later that she opened her eyes during the invitation prayer when she sensed a rustling to her right. Her eyes followed him down the aisle, her lips parting in a smile as she nudged her mother to point toward where Herschel had now reached the pastor standing nearest their seats. After church, they joined the reception line to welcome him into God's family and the First Baptist family. One of his professors stood in line to shake his hand and offer congratulations. Officer Larry Gaines told him it was the best decision he had ever made. Susan's father invited him to lunch to share his journey to faith with his family.

During lunch with Susan and her family, Herschel spilled his story. He didn't leave out anything of substance except his current address. The plight of his childhood saddened them, his path to Millsaps intrigued them, and his business ventures fascinated them. Susan's father pulled him aside later to inform him he might be in the market for a new porch swing. Herschel reached the part of his story concerning his current spiritual quest as they ate apple pie in the sunroom. Over the course of conversation, he learned Susan was an only child, her father was an insurance agent, and her mother was a secretary at the phone company.

Herschel returned to his treehouse late Sunday night, thoughts of salvation and Susan and his future flooding his mind. He stepped over the fence without the aid of his flashlight or any light from the moon. He counted the steps across the grass lane to the treehouse ladder and clambered up to settle in for a long night's sleep. Tomorrow morning, he would sleep in and read his Bible until it was time to meet Mr. Reeves at the physical plant. He crawled across the floor, five steps on his knees, before he reached for his sleeping bag. He stopped cold when his hand touched a pillow at the opening to his sleeping bag.

13

Herschel whipped the flashlight from his back pocket and shone the light around the treehouse. Nothing appeared to have been moved, and the pillow was the only addition to his dwelling. Who knew he was here? He had been careful not to reveal his secret place to anyone. Had a grandchild arrived and left the pillow since his last night in the treehouse? By its position at the top of his sleeping bag, it almost seemed to have been left as a gift. Had a neighbor spotted him coming and going? Had Officer Gaines or Willis Reeves followed him here? Susan or her dad? His blood ran cold at the thought of someone knowing he was here. He sat frozen for the next hour, wondering if he should clear out and not return. At last, he climbed into his sleeping bag, where sleep overtook him with his head nestled into a stranger's pillow.

Herschel could have kicked himself when he woke the next morning to sunlight peeking in through the treehouse opening. Taking a quick glance around the base of the treehouse and seeing nothing out of the ordinary, he began his descent.

"Good morning, Herschel," a voice from underneath the treehouse called.

Herschel stopped on the second rung from the ground, his eyes adjusting to the bright morning light filtering through the branches of the stately oak. A man who looked to be in his mid- to late-sixties and vaguely familiar smiled at him. He offered no ill intent, so Herschel lowered himself to the ground, taking his time to meet the man's extended hand with a reluctant handshake. It was a handshake that conjured a memory Herschel couldn't quite place.

"My name's Jerry Bradford. So you're the young man making himself at home in my treehouse?" Ah, the homeowner that he had only seen from too great a distance to recognize up close. His tone didn't come across as an accusation.

"Yes, sir. I'm sorry, sir."

Bradford waved him off. "It's about time somebody used it. I once promised my son I'd build him a treehouse, and I guess I didn't get around to it in time. Once he grew up and had a boy of his own, I had time to build one, so I built this one for my grandson. Now, they live out of state and if his mother and I want to visit with them, we have to go to Missouri. It's just been sitting here for the last four or five years, waiting for somebody to come along and play in it."

"How..."

"How did we realize someone was living in our treehouse? Well, Gladys—that's my wife—she and I sit out on the back patio at night when the weather is nice like it has been these last few days. Weird winter we're having—we're usually cooped up inside until March by now. Anyway, I slipped around the corner to do my business by a tree out back, and a bit of light from the treehouse caught my eye. That was a week ago. I said something about it to a police officer who goes to church with us, and he had a sneaking suspicion about who it was and told me he thought our guest was harmless. I left the pillow up there a couple of nights ago, but you didn't come. It was nice outside again last night, so I walked around and saw your light. I hope you enjoyed a decent pillow instead of whatever you've been using. You know, Herschel, we've actually met before."

"I thought you looked familiar, and I wondered how you knew my name." Herschel hesitated to say more.

"You were meeting so many people at the time that I doubted you would remember me."

"You were at First Baptist yesterday?"

"Lifelong members. My police officer friend came over afterward and told me he thought I had just met my treehouse guest."

"Was that Officer Gaines?"

Mr. Bradford grinned. "That's him. He's in the Sunday school class I teach."

"Am... I... am I in trouble?"

"No, no, heck, you're welcome to stay until school starts back as far as I'm concerned. The missus would like to meet you as an actual person and not a middle-of-the-night treehouse guest, though. She has bacon and sausage already cooked, and she'll start scrambling some eggs as soon as we turn the corner up there." He pointed to the bend in the landscaping that Herschel had thought of as his safety barrier. "If you're willing to come eat a hot breakfast and chat with a couple of old folks, that is."

"Mr. Bradford, if I'm not in trouble for trespassing on your place, I'd be glad to join you and Mrs. Bradford for breakfast."

Mr. Bradford grinned and reached for Herschel's shoulder to point him toward the house. "Come on, then. I can't wait to hear the story of how a college boy came to live in my treehouse."

BREAKFAST with the Bradfords turned into a conversation much like the one with Susan and her parents the previous day and the one with Reeves a couple of weeks before. With the Bradfords, though, he did not need to hide his living arrangements. After two hours of telling his story, Herschel brought it to a close. When he told them about meeting Susan and how his interest in her led to his pursuit of a relationship with God, Gladys expressed her disapproval.

"So you got saved to impress a girl?"

"Oh, no ma'am. I understand how it sounds, but if I never saw Susan again, my decision to give my life to the Lord would stick."

She relaxed a bit at his response. "Well, I hope so. I can't tell you how many times I've seen a young lady fall for a boy when she thinks he's moving toward God when his motive is to do whatever it takes to win her over."

"Well, that's not me. I think I could fill a notebook with all the questions I have so far from reading the Bible, but I have been reluctant to ask Susan for that very reason. I'm not sure why, since I have so little experience with a relationship with God or a relationship with a girl. Living in a boys' home through high school made it awkward to have a girlfriend. I was so focused on beating the odds and getting to college, I didn't think about girls as much as the average high school boy, I guess."

Mr. Bradford stood and stretched. "Now, about this living arrangement of yours…"

Here comes the hammer, Herschel thought, the end of his time in the treehouse. The seat of his truck might make for a more comfortable bed, but with his clothes and tools in the cab, it would make for cramped living quarters. "Yes, sir?"

"Weather man says that the weather is going to get pretty rough this week, freezing temperatures and a chance of snow."

"Yes, sir, I'll get my stuff out of your treehouse and get a room down at the Sun-n-Sand. That's my home away from… Anyway, I'm sorry about making myself at home in your treehouse."

"Herschel, we would love for you to make yourself at home, but a treehouse is not the best place for us to show you southern hospitality. After all, Mississippi is the Hospitality State. What would you think about moving into the house with us until your dormitory at school re-opens?"

The offer flabbergasted Herschel. "You would do that? But why? You just met me."

"Here's the way it works around here: I'm not a big fan of a big ol' empty house, and I've been ready to move somebody into one of the extra rooms for a while now. Gladys—she's a keen judge of character, so if you get out of line, she'll be able to tell, and we'll make other arrangements. As it is, though, you are welcome to move in for the rest of your break. We ask that you abide by some common courtesy toward us like telling us about your comings and goings, just like you would in a regular fam—"

"What?"

"Herschel, I'm so sorry."

"For what?"

"For assuming you recognize how a regular family works."

"Oh." Herschel's dejected response brightened as he reminded himself of the opportunity sitting in front of him. "I might not understand how a regular family works, but I'm teachable. If you're willing to instruct me, that is. I have imagined raising a family—no time soon, mind you—and I don't know enough about what that looks like. I would be very thankful if you would teach me."

Gladys stared at her husband and then at the vagabond college student standing in her living room. "Young man, you don't realize how much that request means to my husband. Our boy wasn't very receptive to our efforts to teach him how to be a respectable husband and father. Oh, he does all right, I suppose, but not because he was open to much that we had to teach him. Jerry wanted someone to mentor, to disciple, but he didn't know how to make that happen."

Jerry nodded. "Turns out, all I needed to do was build a treehouse and wait for the right drifter to come along and inhabit it."

"Another thing, young man," Gladys added, "if you want a place to invite your new friend, she is welcome here anytime. We have known her since she was born. Her parents, too, for that matter."

"So that worked out for you, then?"

"Better than worked out. Mr. Jerry was an early riser like me. For the rest of my break, we would go into this little sunroom they had off the back of the house where we wouldn't wake Mrs. Gladys, open our Bibles, and talk. I never ran out of questions. Even though he didn't always have the answers I was looking for, he helped me get a big picture perspective of the Old Testament and then the New Testament."

"All over the next two weeks?"

"Pretty much. We talked for hours at a time. He was retired, and I didn't have anywhere to go until the middle of the afternoon. It was like God had been weaving our paths for years to intersect at that particular juncture. I was a new believer and hungry, and Mr. Jerry hoped the Lord could still use him in his later years. We would study and talk about life until Mrs. Gladys called us for breakfast. You might say that we went from a figurative feast on the Word every morning to a literal feast at her table. If I wasn't already developing a taste for Southern food, I certainly did then. I never took to greens or boiled cabbage, but I liked pretty much everything else she cooked."

"What about Susan?"

"Well, after I moved into the house, I asked them not to say anything to Susan's folks so that I could tell them that part of my story over lunch the next Sunday. They had already invited me back, and I felt like my story was incomplete without that minor part. I went, and since I had a place to ask Susan to then, we took up company pretty regular for the next two weeks. Then, she returned to school in Raymond—that was about a thirty-minute drive from her house—and I went back to Millsaps. We wrote letters every Tuesday so that we would have something to read mid-week, and she drove home most weekends. We were dating steady by the time she returned from school in May and talking marriage by the next summer. The Bradfords invited me to stay with them during spring break and during the summer. It was on one of those summer nights that I told Mr. Jerry something about my plans that I had not told anybody, even Susan."

"BEAUTIFUL WEATHER we're having this afternoon, Herschel." Herschel had just pulled in the driveway from his summer construction job for which one of Jerry Bradford's Sunday school class members had hired him. Jerry was pulling the three or four weeds that had somehow avoided his regular surveillance in the flower bed between the house and the driveway. "Mighty cool for this time of year. Y'all might have had this kind of weather in the summer in Michigan, but it's usually hot and humid by this time of year here."

"I appreciated not sweating by just stepping outside, that's for sure."

"You and Susan have any plans for tonight?"

"No, sir, she is going to spend some time with some of her high school girlfriends. We are going on a picnic tomorrow to take advantage of this beautiful weather."

"Wonderful. Where are you taking her?"

Herschel laughed. "To the grass lane leading up to the treehouse. You and Mrs. Gladys are welcome to join us."

"Wouldn't dream of it. Tell you what, though. I had a crazy idea you might could help me with."

"Anything. What did you have in mind?"

14

"I might regret it tomorrow, but doggone it, I built that treehouse so I could spend some time out there with my son and grandson, and now it just sits there empty except when you were using it. I was wondering if perhaps you and I could spend the night out there tonight—have a campout?"

"Mr. Jerry, I can't imagine anything I would rather do. The whole time I lived there, I dared not invite a guest, but it sure got lonely up there sometimes. Not that I had anyone in mind to invite, mind you, since all of my school friends were spending a month with their families."

"I was hoping you would say yes. I took a trailer full of old wood back there earlier this afternoon. We can build a bonfire and roast wienies and marshmallows, tell ghost stories, and just enjoy a big ol' time."

Herschel was tickled at his host's boyishness. "Mr. Jerry, do you know any ghost stories?"

The older man's face broke into a huge grin. "I suppose I could come up with one or two. At the very least, we can swap some Holy Ghost stories. One other thing I want to discuss: I'd like to know how you passed the time up there, what kind of ideas crossed your mind during those lonely hours."

"I'll be glad to fill you in. Mostly business ideas and some plans for how I want to lead my company one day. Until the night I met Susan," he added with a sheepish grin.

"Well, you go get cleaned up from work, and I'll get the fire started. If you don't mind, stop by the kitchen on your way out to the treehouse. Gladys will prepare everything we need for our campout. Take your time, now. It may take me a while to get the fire hot enough for us to cook. You ever been to a wienie roast, Herschel?"

"Yes, sir, that's one thing we used to do all the time at the boys' home. Our house father found that teenaged boys, fire, and food made for perfect entertainment on a Friday night."

"So it does."

An hour later, Herschel pushed a wheelbarrow loaded with food to the makeshift campsite. For the next two hours, the two men—separated by five decades—ate hot dogs and marshmallows and swapped stories near the fire. Herschel shared more specific glimpses of his hurts and triumphs, and Jerry revisited his own college years and how markedly different they were than his young guest's. Their conversation dwindled along with the fire.

"Ready to head up?" Jerry asked.

"Yes, sir. You sure you want to do this?"

"I'm ready—well, almost ready. Where's your bathroom?"

Herschel pointed to the double trunk pin oak thirty feet past the treehouse tree. "Guess I'll go, too."

"I'll take the right trunk, and you take the left trunk."

After taking care of business, the men put out their fire and climbed the ladder up the tree. Hershel paused at the entrance when he saw two sleeping bags spread out and four battery-powered lanterns Jerry was switching on to light the treehouse. He also spotted two glorious pillows that would sure beat a rolled-up sweatshirt for resting their heads.

"I realize you didn't have the benefit of light other than your flashlight," the older man said, "but I didn't think we needed to re-create your entire experience, if that's okay."

"Fine with me. I'd be in my sleeping bag by now," Herschel said. "It was pretty cold some of those nights. I would hunker down until I was warm, and that's when I would doze off. I would wake up most mornings when I heard the papers thunking on the driveways. That was usually between three and four o'clock. I'd gather up my stuff and take it to my truck and crank up the heater. When it was good and warm, I'd turn off the ignition and nap until the cold woke me up again. Nobody ever bothered me."

"On nights when the weather was nice, what did you do? What did you think about?"

Herschel reached for his knapsack that he had tossed on the floor near his sleeping bag, removing his old general business textbook and page after page of notes. He offered them to Jerry.

"What's this?"

"Notes about how I'm going to run a business when I finish school. How I'm going to build it slowly so I don't carry much or any debt. How I'm going to hire employees and train them and keep them loyal to the business. How we're going to treat our customers. How I'm going to show my appreciation to my employees and customers. How I'm going the use the profits from the business to help foster kids like me go to college."

Jerry stared hard at Herschel when he paused. "Young man, I know plenty of men who owned their own businesses for many years, and none of them had the vision that you do. You've got me wanting to buy from you, and I don't even know what you're selling. What do you plan to sell?"

Herschel stood, extended his arms, and turned his head deliberately from one side of the treehouse to the other, a smile forming on his face. "This."

"A treehouse?"

"More than a treehouse. I'm going to sell the experience of a treehouse."

"Well, I'm honored you would want to build my treehouse. Would you sell the plans or build them yourself?"

"Both. For a dad with the skills to build it, what better father-son time can a dad create than building something like this for his son? Better yet, *with* his son. I wish I could have helped my dad build something like this."

"Your idea sounds good, but it didn't work out so well for me and my son."

"I thought about that. What if you had built it when he was still eight, nine, ten years old?"

"It may have made a difference since children tend to be more impressionable at those ages. Now, he's gone and almost never comes back." Jerry's countenance dripped sadness and regret.

Herschel was still in the midst of his dream. "Yes, but remember what we read this morning?"

"The story of Gideon's army."

"And Gideon had how many soldiers?"

"Three hundred."

"Against how many Midianites?"

"Over a hundred thousand. What's your point?"

Ignoring the question, Herschel continued, "So three hundred defeat over a hundred thousand. A prophet and a widow and her child live for many days on enough for one last meal. Five thousand men, plus women and children, eat from five loaves and two fish. A dead man is raised to life. How are all these stories connected?"

"Evidently, that you've been paying attention to our studies."

"Yes, sir. But with all due respect, have you been paying attention, Mr. Jerry?"

"What do you mean?"

"How are all these stories connected?"

"God delivered when hope seemed lost—is that what you're prompting me to say?"

"Say it again."

"God delivered when hope seemed lost."

"Is He still the same God?"

"Yesterday, today, and forever."

"Well, if He did all those miraculous things, and He's still the same God, why can't you imagine His changing your son's heart toward you?"

Jerry's head fell between his knees. "Lord, I hear you speaking loud and clear through this young man at this moment in this place. I confess I didn't hear You through Your Word, but it's right there. You are mighty and I've let my human disappointment make you smaller than You are. Lord, my son doesn't want a relationship with me, and that's my fault for not investing in him when he was younger. It's going to take another mighty work from you, Lord, but I won't stand in Your way anymore by trying to guilt him into a relationship with me. I believe you are the same God who did the mighty works that Herschel talked about and so many more. Our relationship is one touch from You away from being restored. I believe You can, and that You want to bring us back together. I'm asking, Lord—I'm asking that you restore us in Your time and to Your glory. In Jesus' name I pray. Amen."

"Amen."

"Thank you, Herschel. It took courage for you to correct an old man."

"You're welcome."

Silence permeated the treehouse as the last vestiges

of daylight disappeared outside. The temperature was chilly for June in Jackson, Mississippi. As the church clock in the distance struck nine, Jerry reached for a light jacket he had brought in anticipation of the cool night air. "You suppose you can sell enough treehouses to make a living?"

"Treehouses themselves? No. But I'm certain I can sell enough adventure, relationships, and peace to sell thousands of them."

"Now you're talking. Herschel, I'm of the opinion that you're a natural salesman but not one who is out to sell people something they don't need."

"Right, I don't want to convince people they need one of my treehouses. I want to convince them they need a place to retreat, so to speak, and a place to have adventures and for especially fathers to build relationships with their sons."

"Adventures and relationships you didn't have with your dad."

"Right. That's why one of my goals for my company is to become so profitable that I can build one of these for free at every boys' home in the United States."

"That's a noble goal. I would consider it an honor to help you achieve it."

"You already are."

"Me? How?"

"By mentoring me like a father would his son. And this adventure tonight—I never even met my dad, much less did anything like this with him."

"Remind me how old you are."

"Nineteen."

"Remarkable. You seem to have considered all the important parts of running a business that the number crunchers miss. You won't get much of this in your business classes, you understand."

"I realize that. But I need to learn the business side of it so I don't cost people their livelihoods by my ignorance." After a long silence, Herschel added, "Mr. Jerry, I possess a secret weapon that will give me a leg up in the treehouse business."

"Yeah? What's that?"

"I've lived in a treehouse. I embody the story of adventure I plan to sell."

Both men laughed and talked deep into the night about Herschel's vision for his treehouse company. After agreeing they should get some sleep, they both lay quiet for over an hour, neither of them sleeping. Jerry broke the silence. "Do you have a name for this company of yours? Perhaps 'Herschel's Houses?'"

"That would be a good one, but I already chose a name. It's not very catchy, for sure, but it means a lot to me, and it will inspire my work. Two old black men who could have ignored me or even feared me chose instead to mentor me to work with my hands. They taught me to do the little things right and to consider the person I'm building something for while I'm making a swing or a bookcase or anything else. So I'm going to call my company Mitchell-Reeves Adventures."

"I love it."

"It will help honor Mr. Mitchell's memory and make sure the world doesn't forget him. And Mr. Reeves—if it hadn't been for him taking a shot on a nosy college kid,

I'm not sure I would have made it. I had the money to afford to live, especially with my accommodations here, but I'm not sure I could have stood the loneliness of a month by myself. Mr. Jerry, may I show you something else?"

"Of course."

Herschel turned on the lantern near his head and dug through the notes in his business textbook until he found the one he was looking for, a sketch of a treehouse with its measurements. He handed it to the closest thing to a father he had ever known.

"What's this—that's my treehouse."

"The first one I'll offer. I call it *The Bradford*."

DUMBFOUNDED, David said, "You own Mitchell-Reeves Adventures?!?"

Perdue grinned. "You recognize the name."

"Mr. Perdue, when I was growing up, I used to look at your catalogs and dream about what it would be like to own a treehouse where I could plan adventures. I used to dream about what it would be like to have a dad I could enjoy those adventures with. I can't believe I just randomly met you here today. You have no idea."

"David, I stopped believing things happened randomly a long time ago. I'm sorry you never got your treehouse. But you have a relationship with your dad now, right? At least to some level?"

"Yeah, we talk often. I'm not sure I'd call it a deep relationship yet, but I love him, and I can tell he loves me. I'm open to more, but he's been cool with not trying to push too hard. Plus, he is so smitten with my mom that I'm not sure when their honeymoon phase will end. None of my family is in a hurry for it to slow down after twenty-plus years without him. I understand I'm talking in circles. Let's just say I'm hopeful but not pushing for experiences like that with my dad."

"Tell you what. If you two ever get to where you're ready for that father-son adventure, my company runs a retreat center with some of the finest treehouses you've ever seen as our cabins. No girls allowed, just fathers and sons or boys with mentors. We built many other adventures like ropes courses and rock walls and things like that. You and your dad ever want to come, you would be my guests."

"Thank you," David said, shaking his head. "I still can't believe I'm talking to you. Your work is amazing, and your catalogs were an adventure in themselves. I read them from cover to cover every year. The stories of how you built the houses were my favorite, but I thought it was awesome how you invested in fathers and sons, even though I didn't have a father around then. I imagine I transferred many of your business practices to my company without even recognizing I was doing so. It is such an honor to meet and talk to you. How did you end up here?"

"Whoa, slow down there, young fella. That's too big a leap. We've got to put some stepping stones in place to get us from the treehouse to the retirement house."

"Sorry, I'll be patient. I just can't believe I'm talking

to the creator of Mitchell-Reeves Adventures. Did people ever ask you if you were Mitchell or Reeves?"

Perdue roared with laughter, snorting as he rocked back in his chair. "Oh, my goodness, yes, at least once a week. Of course, they naturally assumed that I was one, and the other was my partner. I would ask which one they'd rather talk to, and they wouldn't know what to say to that. After I enjoyed a little fun at their expense, I would tell them my story and how Mr. Mitchell and Mr. Reeves impacted my life and my career. Of course," he added with a wink, "if they had just read the catalog like some people, they would have already known that."

"I know, right? I'm surprised your story didn't sound more familiar to me, but I haven't picked up one of your catalogues in close to ten years. Tell me, did Mr. Bradford's son ever come around?"

"He did, but it took some time. Mr. Jerry was eighty when his son came back and apologized to him for the way he had ignored him for so many years. In his apology, he said he understood there was no way to recover lost time, but Mr. Jerry told him a perfect place to start. Within a week, his son came back with his son, who was a teenager by then. The three of them spent the night in the treehouse together, swapping stories and making up for lost time. Mr. Jerry called me the next day and told me all about it. He died a few years after that, but they spent other nights in the treehouse while Mr. Jerry could still climb the ladder. His son lives in the main house now and enjoys adventures in the treehouse with his son and two grandsons."

"It must have been built sturdy to still be intact."

"Built for generations of adventures, just like all our products."

"That's your tagline."

"Since I started the company over forty years ago."

15

"So things started turning around for you during your first year of college?" David asked.

"They did. I kept working and saving, started taking classes during the summer, and graduated in three-and-a-half years. Mr. Jerry was right—my college professors didn't teach me very much about practical ways to run a small business in my degree program at school. I learned plenty from him, though. It's funny, the reporters who wrote articles on our success focused on my business degree from Millsaps as the key to our success. In reality, it was the free advice of several older men who invested themselves into me that made Mitchell-Reeves what it has become."

"Tell me how you started doing custom treehouses for people."

Perdue adjusted to a more comfortable posture on his couch as he faced David's chair in the retirement home library, where they remained the only visitors. "I arrived in south Mississippi with twenty thousand dollars to start my business, half that I had saved through summer jobs and swing sales and half that Mr. Jerry and Mrs. Gladys gifted me when I graduated. I tell you, David, I didn't want to take that money. They had done so much for me, given a homeless foster kid a place in their home. They never said it out loud, but I think I was like their second chance to raise their own son. Something else that was also no small thing—they gave me a place to court the love of my life.

"Here's the thing that made me comfortable in taking the money from the Bradfords: They believed in me and the vision I had for the business. Of course, they vested themselves on a personal level, too, since it was their treehouse that inspired me to make them for a living. When I handed Mr. Jerry's check back to him, he said—and I can remember it as clearly as if he said it two minutes ago—'Herschel, this is a gift to you. More important to me, it is an investment in the adventure, relationships, and peace you are going to give fathers and sons.'

"Susan and I married at First Baptist Jackson in the chapel. She told me from the beginning she wanted a small wedding. I never knew for sure if that's what she had always wanted or if she shifted gears in deference to my family dynamic. If we had chosen an elaborate summer wedding, her side would have been full, and mine would have been empty. I would have had to include everybody I knew in the wedding party. As it was, Mr. Jerry was my best man, and Susan's best friend was her maid of honor, and that was it. The Bradfords threw us a reception at their house, and we were off to the Peabody in Memphis for our honeymoon. That was courtesy of Susan's parents, who gave us a nice trip since they didn't have the expense of a big wedding. We spent a week in Gatlinburg and then moved down here to Harriston for Susan to start her practice teaching.

"I'll cut through the next stage in our lives, but suffice it to say that I constructed all of two treehouses during that first semester we lived in Harriston. I built swings and bookcases on the side and sold several of those. Our living expenses were minimal, but we stayed so busy that we didn't want for much. When Susan graduated, we researched a better place for me to start over. We settled on Birmingham—magnificent views from a treehouse in the hills of Birmingham, a more affluent population, better opportunities for Susan's teacher salary to carry us while my business got up and running."

David shook his head. "All my years of reading your catalog, I never knew you were so close to me in the beginning. It should be a historical landmark."

"I would be happy to take you to Birmingham and show you what our home office has become over the years. You wouldn't have been much impressed with my home office here in Harriston. Susan and I rented a tiny house just outside of town because it had a shop out back. Your tour would have taken about five minutes."

"How long did it take Mitchell-Reeves to get— excuse the expression—*off the ground* in Birmingham?"

"Well, with Susan earning a salary that would take

care of most of our basic needs, I rented an old ware-house that the real estate agent was more than willing to give me a deal on. Considering it had sat vacant for over two years, she was happy to lease it at almost any price. It was a small warehouse, but enormous compared to what I needed. The key aspect of that warehouse was that it wouldn't gobble up the rest of my start-up money right off. Not to mention that expansion was possible without having to find a new place. I set up my shop and went to work looking for the best places to market my vision.

"I chose the Vestavia Hills neighborhood at the top of Shades Mountain and began spending two hours every evening walking door to door, handing out flyers, and talking to folks. They were friendly enough, but not too interested in my services. I was going to give it three weeks and try the process in another neighborhood. Well, on the Thursday of the third week, I got a bite. It was a couple in their fifties, empty nesters after raising four kids who were now raising kids of their own. They still hosted family lunch there every Sunday and spent most holidays at their house. The adults were all University of Alabama graduates and huge football fans, so their home reflected that. They thought adding a Bama treehouse would be awesome for their growing extended family.

"I spent the next week drawing plans for their tree-house and scouring the UAB campus for strong college boys to hire to put this thing together once I had all the pieces cut. We built it, and it looked nice, but the finishing touches catapulted mine from a solo operation with some part-time help to a bona fide company. This was an upscale neighborhood, so I dared not do anything gaudy, but I cut two big University of Alabama *A*'s, painted them crimson, and positioned them on either side of the door to the treehouse. Let me tell you, that family was ecstatic about that treehouse, and it didn't take long for orders to roll in for 'The Bear.' I named it after Coach Paul 'Bear' Bryant, who coached at Alabama then and was already a legend. By the end of the year, I had built six more Bears and hired three full-time workers to construct them. Another advantage to working in Birmingham is that there were enough breaks in the weather during the winter that we kept going. When springtime came, we added two more models that we could pre-cut and have up within a month. The spring and summer were crazy busy, and we've never looked back. I started getting calls from all over Alabama from folks who wanted 'The Bear,' and we kept rolling from there."

"Sounds like everything was perfect."

"It wasn't."

"HERSCHEL, I'm going to my parents' house for the weekend, maybe longer."

"Longer?" It was Friday at the start of Susan's first summer break. Her first year of teaching full-time in Birmingham had been fantastic, as far as he surmised.

He had been out of town much of that first year, trying to handle the explosive growth of Mitchell-

Reeves Adventures and excited about his sooner-than-expected success. The spring had demanded five days a week for construction and another for planning upcoming projects, which meant traveling across the region. Between construction and planning, he ordered materials, built his expanding workforce, and followed up on completed projects. He discovered his business plan worked as he had believed it would, but he had underestimated the time necessary for over-the-top customer service. He couldn't do it all as well as he would have liked, and his marriage felt the brunt of it. The only consistent time he and Susan had spent together was at church Sunday morning and lunch afterward. Their conversations tended toward his upcoming projects and the lesson plans she worked so hard to prepare for her third-grade class. When she shared her classroom struggles and joys, his mind drifted to treehouses. She noticed.

During spring break, he had invited Susan to visit some of his current treehouse projects with him. She declined, citing a need to drive to Jackson to visit her parents and friends she hadn't seen since Christmas. It should have been telling that she left on Friday afternoon after school and didn't return until the following Sunday afternoon. With lesson plans due the next morning, she had laid right into her work. Herschel noticed but continued working on a new design he was excited to introduce in the coming weeks. They returned to their routines, living separate lives under the same roof. Susan had noticed the drift before Herschel. The word *longer* opened his eyes.

"Longer, I expect." She cried so hard when she tried to explain that her words were no longer coherent. Herschel reached to hold her, but she pushed him away with a defiance he had never experienced from her.

"Susan, please! Tell me what's wrong."

Pulling herself together in a concentrated ball of fury, she exploded. "You figure it out! You're so smart, you figure it out!"

"DID YOU FIGURE IT OUT?"

"David, I had it figured out by the time her car turned out of our driveway. Of course, I wanted to chase her down, explain myself and my plans that already recognized the demands on my time would be a problem in the future. I just didn't know that the future was six months earlier than anticipated, and I had waited too long to make a move. I understood that for Susan's and my future and for the future of the business, I needed to hire a project manager. Since Susan was still in her first year of teaching and working as hard as she was, I put it off, thinking it was better for her if I stayed busy, too. I couldn't have been more wrong or more blind to how far we had already drifted apart.

"Of course, those were the days before cell phones, so calling her and trying to reason with her while she drove wasn't an option. What I wanted to do was jump in my car, chase her down, and convince her to come back home with me. Instead, I stayed and spent that

Saturday interviewing project managers. I ended up hiring one of my own carpenters who had done an outstanding job building the treehouses and who I trusted to lead a crew. We finished in the middle of the afternoon, and I drove up to stay with the Bradfords on Saturday night. After spending several hours the next morning talking to Mr. Jerry and letting him help me figure out what to say to Susan, I drove to First Baptist and arrived right on time for the 11:00 service. I slipped in and sat next to Susan before she could cut and run.

"She tried to act like I wasn't welcome, but she couldn't suppress a little smile. A woman likes to know she's still worth chasing, my boy, and Susan was sure worth chasing. When the time came for folks to greet one another, I leaned over and whispered that I was sorry. I informed her I had hired a project manager to free me up to be home with her much more often. And then I told her that if she would come home with me and give me a week to get Abe started in his new role, I would take her on a vacation. We would then agree on a more viable plan for living in harmony with one another."

"Did she go?"

"She did, and we moved around to the same side of some of our problems and worked through them together. We started having regular date nights, started reading the Bible together in the morning like Mr. Jerry and I used to do, and even started asking each other's perspectives on our work. Every year, we returned to the beach during the first week of her summer break to work out the kinks and make sure we were okay with one another. Some years were peaceful, and to be honest with you, some years hurt so bad I wish I hadn't gone."

David looked surprised.

"You see, David, it was our second year at the beach that we decided we wanted to have children. Susan could still teach but also spend her breaks at home with however many children the Lord decided we should have. I feared having children because of my background. Even with Mr. Jerry's mentoring in my hip pocket, I questioned my competency to be a dad. It stayed in the back of my mind that my dad had taken his life when he became overwhelmed by the idea of raising me alone. Granted, life dealt the man a horrible hand, but no one promised me life wouldn't give me a similar hand. Susan convinced me that whatever struggles I had, I should take them to the Lord, which I don't have any evidence my dad ever did—I just don't know. Plus, she said, as long as the Bradfords were around, I had them and her parents to lean on, too.

"I came around and we started trying. A year passed, then two, then three. People didn't talk about infertility very much in those days, so we felt more and more isolated from our friends who were having children—most of them, multiple children. One year at our beach debrief, we fell into pointing the finger at one another for our failure. Both of us regretted it a day later, but we had said some pretty hurtful things to one another, and it took quite a while—several years, in fact—before we completely recovered from the things we said. We still weren't getting pregnant, and the weight of that was getting heavier and heavier. Susan had it worse than me. She spent nine-and-a-half months of every year teaching and helping raise other folks' children while the yearning inside her to have one grew stronger with each passing year."

"Were you ever able to have children?" David asked, almost too afraid of the answer to ask the question.

Perdue cried, a solitary tear at first but a torrent within the two or three minutes he sat there remembering. David gave him the space, not offering a word but letting him grieve his unspoken sorrow. After a pair of hard sniffles, the older man regained enough composure to speak. His words came out in a hoarse whisper.

"Before I answer your question, my young friend, I need to tell you about my experience with time travel."

"O-kay?"

Perdue laughed. "Don't worry, David Gull, this conversation won't go off the rails. No matter what the staff here may inform you, I am very much in my right mind."

David smiled and encouraged Perdue to continue.

16

"As the years passed without a baby, Susan and I discussed the increasing possibility of being the last members of our respective families. We could have adopted a child. Looking back, it made all the sense in the world, but we wanted our blood carried on to another generation. When that didn't happen for so long, we turned our attention to our family's legacy. If anyone were going to record our family histories so the world didn't forget who we were, it was up to us to write them down. Susan still had plenty of relatives—her parents, her dad's brother, and several cousins on Mr. Taylor's side of the family. Her mother's twin sister still lived in Jackson, along with several aunts and uncles. We set aside a week of her summer break to send her to Jackson. Meanwhile, I booked a flight to Detroit.

"I touched base with Freddy Huffigan, my old house parent at the boys' home. Although his position of authority made him seem old when I lived there, he was only ten years older than I was. I found him in the Michigan phone book, and he remembered me right away. I caught him up to date with my life after my occasional letters to him had ceased after graduation. When I informed him I desired to piece together whatever family history I could find, he jumped at the opportunity to reach out to his contacts in the foster system and assist me. Because he was teaching at a community college then, and he only taught one class on Tuesdays and Thursdays during the summer, he had time to help me. He even offered his guest bedroom—no longer at a home for boys—and I accepted. He picked me up from the airport on a Sunday afternoon, and our quest for the pieces of my past began on Monday morning.

"Freddy—it was weird calling him anything but Mr. Huffigan that first day—did some leg work before I arrived in Detroit, using his contacts in social services to track down some information about my parents. Early Monday morning, Freddy and I loaded his car with the files he had created for our quest for what we expected to be a long, grueling day of street pounding. Our first stop was Edison Avenue, where my parents lived all of their married life. I believe I already told you Dad bought the house and met Mom while shopping for furniture to fill it. So Mom fitted the house in her style even before she agreed to a date with my father. I didn't expect the surreal feeling that came over me when we pulled up to 1172 Edison Avenue or how easy our task of discovering my parents' history would be.

This was 1980, so I hadn't turned twenty-seven yet. The bungalow that sat on a postage stamp lot was my home for the first few turbulent days of my life outside the hospital. This was where my mom delivered the best news of my dad's life and where, nine months later, he made the choice to end it. Those thoughts rushed on me like an unexpected ocean wave as I stared at the well-kept house indwelled by strangers. As I fought through the emotions before reaching for the car door handle, Freddy stayed silent and patient. I considered the ancient proverb that a journey of a thousand miles begins with a single step. The odyssey my first step began felt like more than I could bear until I reached for that door handle. Seconds later, though, I walked up the front walk, climbed the three concrete front steps, and rang the doorbell.

———

"Hello," said a young mother with an infant on her hip.

My breath left me in that moment, but Freddy recognized the situation and stepped forward to introduce me.

"Ma'am, my name is Freddy Huffigan. I used to be a house parent at a boys' home here in Detroit. This young man is Herschel Perdue. He lived there until he graduated in 1972 and moved to Mississippi, of all places, to attend college. He lives near Birmingham, Alabama, now, and… gosh, I'm rambling. Herschel is attempting to piece together his past, and your house belonged to his parents when he was born. We were hoping you could give us some guidance."

"Nice to meet you both," she replied with a pleasant smile. Stepping through the screen door and motioning toward a pair of chairs on the porch, she asked, "Won't you take a seat?" She claimed the porch swing and adjusted her baby boy to her shoulder before she pushed off with her foot to set the swing in motion, a gentle rocking back and forth.

After Freddy and Herschel sat, she introduced herself as Lucy Grayson, wife of Gary Gene Grayson and mother to six-month-old Gary Claiborne Grayson.

Herschel had recovered enough by then to share an abbreviated version of his story. Through the trials in the story of this stranger on her porch, Lucy nodded and groaned as his life story took one sorrowful turn after another. Little Gary dozed in her arms.

"I'm not sure I can help you much with the history of the house," she responded when he finished. "My husband and I bought it from an older couple eight months ago. I wish I could tell you we found a box of letters in the attic that would answer all your questions, but... sorry, no such luck."

Freddy chuckled. "We weren't expecting our search to be that easy. We were hoping for the names and addresses of some neighbors who might have lived here when Larry and Helen lived here. This seems like a stable neighborhood, so perhaps someone remembers them and can point us in a helpful direction."

Lucy smiled and adjusted Gary on her shoulder. "I imagine I can help you with that. This little package in this neighborhood makes for easy introductions. Little Gary has plenty of adopted grandparents here. I'm shy by nature, but the neighbors come up and introduce themselves when I take him for a stroll. I didn't find a box of letters in the attic, but if neighbors are what you're looking for, I have something that will help you. Would you mind holding Gary for a minute?"

Before Herschel could respond, he was doing his best to replicate how Lucy had held her baby. His imagination clicked into overdrive as he imagined his father's awkwardness holding him on this very porch. He hoped one day his own son would nestle under his chin like little Gary was doing now.

"Swap you," Lucy said, thrusting a folded yellow legal-sized paper in Herschel's direction. She took her child back and continued, "I'm terrible with names, and Gary—this one's daddy—is not much better, but that might work out to your benefit. When you're the only ones new to the neighborhood and you have a baby on a street that hasn't seen one in a while, word gets around. Once we met two or three neighbors, the rest of them treated us as though they had already met us, too. You'll see on that sheet the names we have been able to piece together a block in any direction."

Herschel opened the paper to discover much of the information that may have taken days to discover on his own. On a crude aerial drawing of Edison Avenue and its adjacent streets, Lucy had written first and last names on many of the squares representing surrounding houses. On some of those, she had written approximate ages, occupations, length of time in the neighborhood. In pencil, she had jotted reminders of food that many of the neighbors had brought when they moved in and when they brought their baby home. He saw check marks next to dishes to be returned to each.

"I'm impressed with the data you have collected here," Herschel said.

"Like I said, I'm not good with matching names and faces. This helps me identify the neighbors who have shown us such kindness."

"Lucy, would you mind if we borrowed your neighborhood map for a few days while we try to piece together Herschel's parents' life here?" Freddy asked.

"Oh, goodness, yes. You keep it as long as you need. I would like it back, though."

"Tell you what, we'll take it by a copy shop and make duplicates for ourselves. That way, we won't risk losing your hours of research."

Lucy nodded. "Once you get one neighbor to talk to you, word will spread, and the rest of them will come to you. If you want to pick a place to start, I'll make a call and let them know you'll be dropping by for a visit."

"That would be helpful. Herschel only has a few days before he has to fly home to Alabama, so that would expedite our research, for sure."

An hour later, Herschel and Freddy were back with Lucy's original map, their copies in hand. They thanked her for her help and walked three doors down Edison Avenue to Elizabeth Stewart's house. According to Lucy's notes, she was a widow in her late seventies or early eighties. A decades-long resident of the neighborhood, Ms. Stewart had brought the Graysons chess squares on a white platter with red trim and a painted rooster in the middle. They returned the platter three days later. When Gary Claiborne Grayson came home to Edison Avenue, the Graysons received it again—this time filled with brownies. They returned the rooster platter two days later, along with a thank you note.

"HELLO, BOYS, COME ON IN," said a vivacious woman carrying the look and smell of a fresh home perm. "Lucy called and said you might drop by to see me. How about some fresh chocolate chip cookies? I took them from the oven ten minutes ago, so they should be perfect." Herschel and Freddy introduced themselves and reached for the red-rimmed platter as Elizabeth Stewart poured lemonade from a pitcher into three lemon-adorned plastic tumblers. "Gotta have something to wash them down with," she said with a pleasant smile.

After three cookies and two glasses of lemonade apiece, she placed her hands in her lap, satisfied that Freddy and Herschel had appreciated her hospitality. "Herschel Perdue. I didn't think I'd ever lay eyes or hands on you again. I remember holding you as a baby, rocking you for hours while your daddy..." Ms. Stewart trailed off.

"So, Ms. Stewart, you lived here when my parents did?"

"Oh, goodness, yes. I have lived right here in this house forever, it seems. Cy—that's my late husband— and I moved here from east Tennessee a year after we married. Now, you call me Elizabeth since you're all grown up now."

"And you helped take care of me as a newborn?"

"I did. There were a group of six of us who watched after you. Two of them have gone on to be with the Lord, but Suzette, Nancy, Claudette, and I are still kicking. Claudette lives in Florida with her husband now, but Suzette and Nancy live around the corner from where you're sitting right now. The three of us did like your mama and married men a good bit older than us, so we're part of the neighborhood widows' club now."

"I'm sorry," Herschel began before Elizabeth waved him off.

"Don't be. We had forty years or more with our husbands. That's a pretty good run by today's standards. I suspect you didn't come all the way to Detroit from Birmingham to delve into the lives of three old widow ladies, though, did you?"

"No, ma'am," Herschel answered. "I don't mean to cut you off, but my mission this week is to gather as much information as I can uncover about my parents because…" Herschel hesitated.

"Because those of us who knew your parents won't be around much longer?" Elizabeth offered.

"Oh, no, not that at all. The truth is, my wife is an only child like me, and we're struggling to have children. We've decided to track down as much of our family histories as possible in case we're the last of our respective generations. She's in Jackson, Mississippi, this week interviewing her extended family members.

Mine is a taller order with a shorter timetable since I live so far away."

"My goodness gracious, bless your heart." She opened her mouth to say more, but stopped herself.

"I can do the math on my parents' ages and figure they either had the same struggle, or I was an accident."

Elizabeth reached for both of Herschel's hands. "You look me in the eye, young man." When he locked his gaze on her unflinching face, she continued, "Larry Perdue loved Helen Perdue with a fierceness that was striking to anyone paying attention. I remember one of the neighborhood gossips saying one time that a love as resilient as theirs owed the world a child. Herschel, your parents wanted you more than anything." He felt the strength escape Elizabeth's hands when she added, "Except each other. But, rest assured, your mother wanted you. And even though he was overcome with Helen's death, your father did, too."

Herschel sank back into his chair, his firmest belief affirmed. "Then why…"

"Honey, I don't know, other than Helen was Larry's world for so long that when the Lord took her…" Elizabeth shrank back. "Are you sure you want to start down that rabbit hole?"

"Ma'am, child services took me away when I was, what, two weeks old, give or take a few days? I never knew my parents at all, except what I would overhear various social workers say when they didn't think I was listening. The sum of my knowledge for all these years has been that my mother died giving birth to me, and my dad killed himself because he couldn't handle the grief. To be honest with you, I don't know if that last part is true."

Elizabeth nodded. "It's true. Say, I don't know what you boys have planned for the week—Lucy said you would be here all week. If you have time, I feel sure Suzette and Nancy would love to see you all grown up and hug your neck. We could tell you everything our old minds remember about your precious mom and dad. Our families lived in the neighborhood together, attended church together, and such. All the men worked at GM in various capacities. Of course, everybody in Detroit in those days worked for either GM or Ford. Tell you what, Herschel, why don't you plan on coming over for dinner tomorrow night? I'll make sure Suzette and Nancy are here. Freddy, you're welcome to join us, too."

PERDUE THREW his hands behind his head, satisfied he had filled in the blanks of his story. "David, I look back on that trip to Michigan as the first time I met my parents. From conversations my parents had with the neighbors through the years, I learned everything I have shared with you today. I discovered being an only child is something that has run in my family for generations. My dad's grandfather came to Michigan on the first of the orphan trains back in 1854. According to the neighbors, my dad said my great-grandfather called himself the 'leftover child' in a German immigrant family of eleven children that could only afford ten. Are you familiar with orphan trains?"

When David shook his head, Perdue continued. "Orphan trains took children from overflowing orphanages in big East Coast cities like New York and Boston and placed them with families in the Midwest and West. Farm families wanted extra farmhands as much as they did children, many times. Just like the foster system today, many caring families took in these children, and there was also plenty of abuse. Over three-quarters of a century, starting in the mid-1800s, they transferred as many as a quarter million children out of the cities to rural America. The modern foster system got its start with the orphan train movement. Like I said, my great-grandfather was on the very first train that ended up in Dowagiac, Michigan, almost 200 miles west of Detroit. Elizabeth Stewart said like most men of his era, my dad didn't open up about many personal issues, but he was proud to talk at length about August Perdue, my great-grandfather."

"I traced my dad's lineage several generations back through a vigorous combing of old records. My mom's was easier, but I tracked her people all the way back to Germany. I followed up with one of those ancestry sites after I started writing this book, and the research I did back then was accurate. My grandfather, Frank Perdue, was born in 1870, an only child. I can only imagine that August didn't want another 'leftover child,' as my grandfather told my dad he continued to refer to himself. Frank moved his family to Detroit around the turn of the twentieth century, and my father was born not long afterward in 1903. Again, he had no brothers and sisters. And you already know I was an only child, born to Larry and Helen later in life."

"You have a fascinating family history, Perdue."

"Indeed, but I could only scrape together a fraction. Mom's story is interesting, too, but Dad's history seemed more pertinent to my struggles. I met with those three neighbor ladies every other day during my trip to Michigan. They took me to the cemetery where my parents were buried side by side. I sat and talked to their memories for hours. I flew home to Birmingham at the end of the week, feeling like I had a semblance of a relationship with my parents and theirs and theirs before them. Mom and Dad were quiet and reserved, for the most part, but I'm grateful they shared significant parts of their lives with a few trusted neighbors who were still alive to share them with me. All those ladies are long gone now. I'm so happy that Susan pushed me to unearth my past, especially my dad's part of it. I felt like you needed to relive my Michigan trip with me in order to appreciate the next chapter of Susan's and my life."

17

"David, it's funny how life repeats itself. Not laughable funny, but ironic funny. My dad waited until what must have seemed forever for a child. Here I was, twenty-five—thirty-five years later—doing the same thing. When Freddy Huffigan and I met some of my parents' neighbors, they told me how agonizing the wait was for my parents and how my dad told them about the night Mom told him she was pregnant with me. When I thought back to that, I felt his angst, you know, better understood the emotional roller coaster that led to his taking his life. I still think he took a coward's way out, but I experienced some empathy toward him, especially the longer our own efforts dragged on."

"What about your wife? How did she handle waiting to get pregnant?"

"With her usual good humor at first. The longer we didn't have a child, the more sensitive we felt and the more alone we became within our friend group. I mean, we were approaching our thirties with zero friends who were in our situation, wanting to have kids but not having them. Our friends slipped out of our lives a couple at a time. Before long, Susan and I stared across the table at one another without much to say to one another. We stopped talking about our dreams of a family because neither of us wanted to hurt the other. To make things worse, her parents were in poor health, so we recognized time was slipping away for us to give them the grandchildren they wanted, even if they didn't say so. The Bradfords were our haven; we would drive to Jackson just to spend a few hours with them at least once a month. They had no expectations of us except that we hang on to God while we weren't getting what we wanted from Him."

"That's good that you had them."

"*Had* them is right. Within fifteen months in 1979 and 1980, Susan and I lost both of her parents and both of the Bradfords. Wave after wave, I'm telling you."

"Oh, my goodness. Tell me you're kidding."

"I wish I was." Perdue stood and stretched, willing himself through the rough stretch of memories. "Susan's dad went first, of cancer that he had battled for several months. Two months later, Mrs. Gladys dropped dead of a heart attack while she was out working in her garden. Mr. Jerry didn't last a month without her. He passed away in his sleep with a smile on his face, fifteen years after he introduced himself to me at the base of my treehouse hideaway. The next winter, Susan's mother caught a cold that just wouldn't go away. Turns out, she had developed pneumonia, and by the time she went to the hospital, doctors couldn't bring her back."

David couldn't sit still any longer. He stood and paced, his mind trying to wrap itself around the pain that his new friend must have carried. "How did you... I mean..."

"We reminded ourselves to breathe. We reminded the Lord that we had no more strength of our own and that we needed His." Perdue's countenance grew resolute. "And He came through for us. Susan and I counted on one another like we never had before for such an extended period. Our beach trip that year seemed different from what it had ever been. We both sensed it. We held hands on long walks up and down the beach and realized more than ever that everybody around us didn't recognize the depth of pain we were attempting to purge. It was just the opposite of my window here: fine on the outside but broken on the inside. It occurred to both of us that our situation at the beach was a microcosm of our situation back home. We had drifted so far from people at work and church that we had become distant from everything and everyone that once gave us purpose and hope for our future. It was a depressing realization.

"Near the end of our trip, we were sitting on some beach chairs at the edge of the gulf, dangling our toes in the water. We had been quiet for a long time, nothing unusual for us as sunset approached, but I knew what she was thinking, and I'm pretty sure she understood what was going through my mind. I sneaked a peek at Susan and said, 'Come work with me.' She looked back at me, smiled, and said nothing more than, 'Okay.' We watched the sun set and returned the chairs back to our beach house. That's when she asked me what I wanted her to do. I flipped it on her and asked what she wanted to do. She said she wanted to start a non-profit arm of Mitchell-Reeves to speed up building our treehouses at children's homes all over the country. There she stood, as beautiful as ever, my dream come true, asking to make my business dream come true. I've never loved her more than at that moment.

"After we settled on how to move forward in our silent grief, it's like the floodgates opened for us—in a good way, I mean. You remember what the view looked like through that broken pane before you took it out and replaced it with the new one? From the inside, I mean."

"Yes, sir. You could see through the inner pane fine, but the outside wasn't clear. Your view was distorted."

"That's it. That's the way Susan and I viewed the world. Our inability to produce a child was the rock slung into our window. And the people who best understood our inner broken pane were all gone. When I thought to ask her to come on board with my company and she agreed, though, it was like God took out the broken pane and let us see through a clear window again. The ideas He had for our marriage came on like a torrent. We accepted where we were, alone, and the last branches of our family trees. After we did that, God opened our eyes to needs we could meet all around us. We came home and visited retirement homes—they weren't as nice as this one—but lonely is lonely, whether the coffee is gourmet or store brand. We made friends in our church with some older empty nesters who were trying to adjust to life as a couple again. Better than that, Susan and I spent many of our Saturdays visiting one children's home after another and building relationships with them through her non-profit wing of Mitchell-Reeves.

"When I made the move to hire a project manager way back during Susan's and my first year of marriage, it freed me up to work on more custom designs for my treehouses. Those were expensive for the end user, but I was doing them for people who could afford them. I discovered many of my clients were quite generous, too. I would tell them about my vision for building a beautiful treehouse at every children's home possible, and, as often as not, they would pull out their checkbook and pay for one, just like that. Before long, the non-profit side was necessary to make sure we kept that money separate. We called it our New Heights initiative. Susan was a perfect fit to lead it to those new heights.

"By the time Susan decided she wanted to lead that part of our business, she had plenty of resources. All she had to do was convince the leaders of the children's homes to say yes to free treehouses. Within a year of her leading New Heights, we were building unique treehouses all over the South. It didn't take long before many of our weekend scouting trips were by plane instead of by car. It was expensive, but we couldn't outspend our donors. Plus, we continued to funnel a percentage of our profits from the for-profit sales into the non-profit side. And sales were booming. That's when we began telling our company's story through that catalog you loved so much.

"When Susan and I returned to the beach the following summer, we stood amazed at all God had done in a year, in the business, in each of us, and in us as a couple. We had purpose, we had friends—including several couples who joined us at the beach that year—and we had a never ending string of weekend dates all over the country. We were on top of the world. Near the end of our trip, though, we had to adjust our plans for the future.

"I had just come back to our beach house from playing a round of golf one afternoon with some older gentlemen who had joined us for the week. Susan informed me their wives had decided she and I were going to dinner with the others and that I needed to hurry and clean up so we could snag an outdoor table. This restaurant was right on the water, and if you arrived early enough, they let you keep your seats on the deck all the way through sunset. They gave you plenty of time between courses to sit and visit and wait for the sun to go down. It was a delightful experience, and we tried to go there at least once every summer. This would be our first time to try it with friends.

"Well, we grabbed a table, settled in, and started telling stories. You never knew the direction the conversation would turn with this group with whom we had cultivated deep friendships in just the previous year. The rest of the gang was older than us, so we did a lot of listening. On this night they started talking about the sibling rivalries they had seen in their kids, birth order and such. Of course, Susan and I had nothing to add to the conversation since both of us were only children with no kids of our own. We were okay just listening, though, and they told some hilarious stories. That carried us all the way through the main course—always shrimp Alfredo for me—and they switched over to telling how each of them discovered they were pregnant. That wasn't as comfortable a topic for Susan and me. Or perhaps I should speak for myself."

"One by one, they told their stories and pulled out pictures of their oldest to show everybody else. As the conversation moved its way around to Susan, I took her hand under the table and gave it a little squeeze. She smiled back at me to let me know she was okay, but I worried that all the talk of firstborns might dredge up what we had put to rest the summer before. One lady suggested we change the subject, but Susan told everyone we were fine and that she was enjoying their stories, so they kept going.

"When the lady sitting to Susan's left finished her story of telling her husband she was pregnant at his birthday party, it hit too close to home for me. I wanted to run, and I prepared to excuse myself to the restroom, but Susan grabbed my hand and whispered it was going to be okay."

RACHEL WINSTEAD HAD STARTED the conversation and seized the silence after Deborah Tudor passed the photo of her eldest around the table to ask, "Did anyone save room for dessert? I can't wait to sink my teeth into some of that key lime pie!"

"Thanks, Rachel," Susan said in a husky voice that hinted of swallowed emotions, "but I want my turn."

"Okay. I just didn't…"

Susan reached across Herschel to pat Rachel's arm. "I understand, and thank you. Believe me, it's fine. This entire conversation is okay with us. Herschel and I have had the most fabulous year of our marriage, reaching out to kids who don't belong to us, but we love them anyway. I don't have a picture to show you of our oldest, but I drew some pictures earlier this week that I want to show you." She reached into her purse to produce an index card with pencil sketches of a little boy playing with a dog on one side and a little girl playing with a dollhouse on the other. "I drew pictures of what our first child might look like as a toddler." She passed it around the circle, where each person glanced at both sides, silently praying that it would be true.

After studying her friend's face, Rachel dared, "Susan, are… you…?"

Susan beamed.

"Wait, what?!" Herschel exclaimed, jerking his chair back to get a better look at his wife. In doing so, he toppled over and landed on his back, peering up at the faces of the surprised guests at the next table. Scrambling to his feet before slipping and falling again, he apologized to the stranger from whom he couldn't seem to untangle himself. "I think I just found out…" He whipped back around to Susan, who was nodding like crazy as she laughed at her capsized husband. The man at the table Herschel had almost crashed into pumped his hand and offered his congratulations before pulling him up to rejoin his own party. The well wishes continued through key lime pie at sunset.

"OH, man, I feel like I should congratulate you myself!" David said.

"I have attempted to describe my response to Susan's announcement, but even words like *shocked*, *stupefied*, and *flabbergasted* fall short. Many times, I had imagined what my dad must have felt thirty-something years earlier when Mom told him she was pregnant with me. In all my years of trying to understand my dad, I connected with him more in the single moment of Susan's announcement than all other moments combined. In a private moment much later that night, I stared at the ocean from our balcony and muttered, 'I love you, Dad.'"

"So—baby boy or baby girl?"

"David, I can't wait to find out."

18

"September 4, 1984, the Tuesday after Labor Day—
Susan didn't show up for work. She walked in a
few minutes before eight every morning. Her office was
on the opposite side of the warehouse from mine, but
her secretary called mine to find out if I knew where she
was. It wasn't like Susan to come in late without letting
Dot know where she was and when to expect her. Right
away, I sensed deep down in my gut a feeling I can't
explain except to say I felt suddenly separated from her.

"I took off to cover the route from our house to the
office. Susan had talked me into getting a mobile phone
—they were pretty rare back then—so I made my
assistant promise to call me the minute she heard
anything. I wasn't even a mile down the road when she
called and told me to pull over as soon as I was able. She
didn't want me driving when she informed me Susan's
car had collided with an eighteen-wheeler. The highway
patrolman who called the office said the scene hinted of

the driver having fallen asleep at the wheel and crossing over into Susan's lane. The paramedics rushed her to the hospital, but the patrolman's words to my assistant were, 'Don't get his hopes up.'"

DAVID SENSED Perdue's composure fading fast as they both paced the floor of the Winding Acres library. However, the older man persisted. "The doctor met me three steps inside the door. He was a member of my church who had attended my Sunday school class for a time. That helped because when he told me he was sorry, but she was already gone, I collapsed into his arms. I can't tell you how long he held me or much of anything else for days afterward. Her funeral was a blur. To this day I can't remember which person sang what or said what or even who attended her funeral. People packed the church and overflowed into the lobby, they say, but I don't remember. I was still in shock.

"I guess there's a part of me that has never recovered from Susan's death." At this, Perdue succumbed to the pain of retelling the story. David caught him and held him without a word for several minutes until the onslaught of emotion subsided. Releasing him, David saw age he didn't see at first in an otherwise fit man of almost seventy. "I'm so sorry, Mr. Perdue. Thank you for sharing the most hurtful part of your story with me. Trust me, your readers will appreciate your transparency. You never know when someone who is going through something similar might pick up your book and find encouragement that someone else has gone through terrible pain, too."

After one leftover sob, Perdue nodded. "David, I have been through so many challenges in my life that seem unique to me. This one—Susan and our baby's deaths—was so much more overwhelming than the others, though. I didn't just lose a part of me in the wreck; I lost two parts." Perdue noticed the tears in the corners of David's eyes now raced down his cheeks. "I'm not writing this book for anyone to feel sorry for me. Tell me, David, are you sympathizing with me right now?"

"I… well, yes, of course I am. I am overwhelmed by the circumstances of your life. I mean, you have faced a relentless onslaught of sorrow. Anyone with any kind of heart for his fellow man would sympathize with you, I would imagine. How could anyone not feel sorry for you? Not like you're somehow less than, but more like you've faced more than your share of adversity. It almost seems like God was piling on."

"I understand, I suppose, because I felt sorry for myself, for sure. I'm writing my story so maybe someone else who life punches in the gut will find encouragement that God can pull him or her through it, like you said."

Puzzled, David said, "I expect they will. Why is it such a big deal to you that your readers not sympathize with you?"

"Because my greatest regret is how much time and effort I put into feeling sorry for myself. I was thirty-one years old when Susan died, and I spent longer than that in a fog, lost in a pity party, some might say. I poured myself into the business, but I would shut anyone down who wanted to ask how I was doing. In doing so, I closed off some caring people, even lost a couple of their friendships. No, David, I don't want my story to give permission somehow to anyone else walking through grief to respond like I did."

David let the words sink in and swirl around in his mind. "But suppose you wrote that part of your story as an example of what not to do."

"A cautionary tale. Hmm."

"Why don't you tell me about that sizable gap of your life you don't want to write? With all due respect, perhaps I can offer another perspective."

"Not much to tell. I worked six days a week, at least twelve hours a day and traveled as much as possible—to keep moving, you know. I put on a cheerful face when I talked about adventure, relationships, and peace. My vision was so strong when I started my company that I was still able to fake my way through the presentations. You would have been a boy then, living your adventures through our catalogs. All the while, though, I wondered if I was selling people like you and others a bill of goods—like life would snuff out my customers' dreams like it had mine. Still, when I would get letters and, eventually, emails with photos of kids and their parents enjoying my treehouses together, a part of me still connected with the old vision and kept me pushing forward.

"I concluded that if I filled my life with enough work and travel, I might ignore the pain long enough that it would one day go away. I couldn't have verbalized it in those days, but that was my reality. Shortly after Susan died, I hired a housekeeper to keep my house clean. The best part of having her come to the house every day to do housework was the sense that someone besides me had been there. When I drove home to my clean but empty house, though, the loneliness crept in on me the moment I pulled in the garage. So I sold the house and moved. And then I moved again. I sold the Florida beach house without ever going back to it. I bought vacation cottages and cabins and condos all over the country, some gorgeous places, but one thing never changed: the loneliness always tagged along.

"The longer I ran from my grief, the more I considered my dad and how he escaped from the world that had closed in on him. As time passed, it made more sense why he made the choice he did. Thirty years after Susan died, I considered suicide for the first time. That was seven years ago. At first, it was just a fleeting idea I waved off as a passing fancy, and it wouldn't come to mind again for several months. Then, weeks. Then, days. My world was closing in on me as my dad's had on him.

"One weekend, I had escaped to my cabin in Pigeon Forge. The leaves were changing, and the water was flowing under my third-floor deck, where I was sitting with my morning coffee. The sun appeared over the horizon, and the sky was as brilliant with color as the trees. Sane people would have been marveling at such a beautiful, picturesque scene. Most Christians would have been thanking God for sitting them down right in the middle of His glorious creation that morning. Even people who didn't believe in God might have sat where I did, satisfied that their hard work and ingenuity had provided such an opportunity to appreciate the fruits of their labor. Not me. I wondered if a three-story fall into the rocks would suffice to... you know.

"The thought scared me, and I didn't go back to that cabin the next fall when the leaves changed. It didn't matter, though. The next year, I spent a weekend at my Myrtle Beach cottage on the anniversary of Susan and the baby's death. It crossed my mind to stroll into the surf and continue walking into the Atlantic. I'll spare you any more specifics, but those were my thoughts. They became more frequent, more vivid all the time. I don't want to give anyone any ideas, so you see my dilemma?"

"I do," David agreed. "Did you ever..."

"No, I never actually attempted it."

"What stopped you?"

"At first, the determination I maintained not to take the same route my dad had. Ultimately, though, it was a phone call from Dr. Stephen Crossgate, the emergency room doctor who broke the news about Susan and our child to me. I was acquainted with him before the accident but just in passing. He was a young doctor then, one who had visited our church. I sat next to him at a men's breakfast one Saturday morning with no idea that his words would crush my world within a few months.

"Dr. Crossgate moved away to North Carolina for an opportunity to practice at a larger hospital not long after Susan died . He lived in the Carolinas for almost thirty years, married a girl from up there, and raised a family. Life couldn't have been better for his family, but life threw him a curve. His mom was diagnosed with cancer, so he planned to move his family to Birmingham so he could help take care of her. They were all packed up and ready to move, and his wife chose then to break the news to him that she would not be moving to Birmingham with him and their children. So he moved back to Alabama with three teenaged daughters to take care of his ailing mother. That was about a month before he called me."

"Oh, my goodness."

"Hang on, it gets worse. This guy had just turned onto Highway 78—he's just a hundred-and-fifty miles from his childhood home where he would have his family's support as he offered support to his mom—and his cousin called to tell him his mother had a massive heart attack. Before he made it home, she passed away. He didn't even have a chance to say goodbye. Can you imagine that?"

"No, but you could, right?"

"I should have been able to help him, but I had nothing for him except to listen when he called me weeks after all that happened. He asked what grief group I had joined to help work through my pain. I couldn't help this man, David. More than thirty years after Susan died, and I had no answers for myself, much less any words of comfort to offer him. I still believed in God, but I had wandered so far away that I'm not sure I trusted Him anymore. Telling this doctor that God loved him and would help him through his misery seemed like such shallow words, I didn't even try to say them."

"So what happened?"

"Well, I didn't talk to him again for about a year, though I would offer up an occasional prayer for Stephen. That's the best word to describe my prayers at that point in my life: *occasional*. Certainly not fervent or without ceasing like the Bible tells us to pray. Then, I saw Stephen in church one Sunday and reconnected. I had hopped around churches since Susan died and finally found one where I blended in. What I was really doing was losing myself in the crowd. When some churches discover you own a successful business, they give you an extra special welcome, if you know what I mean. Well, this church seemed different, so I felt comfortable there. As comfortable as I would have felt anywhere, that is.

"I looked up one Sunday during the singing, and this doctor and his girls stood several rows up and to my left. He held both hands in the air, worshiping like he was standing before Jesus Himself. I couldn't believe it, so I waited around afterward to re-introduce myself. He remembered me, thanked me for taking his call months earlier, and apologized if his call conjured memories of the bad news he had given me so many years before. I asked how he was doing, and he was honest about how the struggles sometimes over-whelmed him. He said his grief group had helped him to—his words, 'redeem the pain.'

"David, I did a lot of thinking from the time your guy broke my window until you replaced it this morning. This was another period on which I look back and realize I was viewing my circumstances through a broken pane. Before Stephen left me that Sunday morning, he pulled out his church bulletin and pointed to an announcement about a grief support group holding their first meeting the next Thursday night. He said, 'It's never too late. It's only ten weeks, and I would be glad to go with you. It wouldn't hurt me to walk through the process again.' He was offering to take me somewhere to repair the broken pane I couldn't seem to fix by myself. Money had long since stopped being important to me. I had spent much of what I should have been giving away, trying to dull my pain. I told Stephen if he was serious about coming with me, I would see him on Thursday night."

19

"Welcome, Mr. Perdue."

Herschel stepped inside the church's fellowship hall and responded with a formal greeting of his own. "Good evening, Doctor Crossgate."

"Please, call me Stephen."

"And you can just call me Perdue."

"Perdue, huh? Any reason you want to go by your last name instead of your first?"

"Last thing I own that belonged to my parents." Stephen cocked his head to the side and narrowed his eyes. Perdue said, "That's right, I haven't shared my story with you. How about I tell it during the meeting so I can tell it once?"

"Deal. Are you nervous?"

"A little."

"That's normal. Look, we're expecting between six and ten people tonight. Some attend our church and some come from other churches. A few don't go anywhere. We may pick up a few more who didn't sign up for the group, but that's okay. So far, everyone in this new group claims through their paperwork to be a follower of Jesus. "

"Claims to be?"

"Oh, I'm not claiming the ability to judge another person's heart. Several people have given their lives to the Lord during the various grief groups, so we always offer the opportunity. Once people lay their grief aside, they understand needs they didn't see before, and the need for God is the most important one."

"Who is this we you keep referring to?"

"Sorry, I forget sometimes that most folks who show up to grief recovery group don't understand how it works. Most of them, you'll find, are going through their first major loss."

"Not you, though."

The doctor's head tilted forward a little. "No, I guess that's why they asked me to lead. Sorry, there I go again. The church staff sensed a group like this would meet a need in our community. I lead the group most of the time. I'll be here every week, Lord willing, and Pastor Reggie Lambert, the community groups pastor, will be here sometimes. This was his idea. After a drunk driver hit and killed his wife's sister, he felt helpless when he tried to guide her through the overwhelming grief that followed. He shows up once to tell his story and other times to see if there are needs he can help with through individual counseling. We put together a little retreat at the end—a graduation, of sorts—and he gives a wrap-up speech. Anybody is welcome to take part in the group, even if they have been through it already, as long as they complete the entire ten weeks, so we build a trust level with one another."

"Stephen, if you understood the grief I've been carrying, you would realize ten weeks will not be enough for me."

"And that's all right. It takes different people different amounts of time to process their grief. We've found it seems to take less time to process it when it has been longer since a person's tragedy. Grief takes time. Some people try to circumvent the gift God has given us through grief—Pastor Reggie will talk more about that later tonight—and skip some steps." Stephen stopped at the door with a sign that read Grief Support Group. "I'm sorry, I'm running ahead again. What I can promise is if you commit to coming all ten weeks, you will make significant progress. I can't say you'll be healed, but I can guarantee that you'll be better."

"Better would be good." Herschel sucked in and released a deep breath and walked through the door.

When he walked out two hours later, his gait was alive with hope. He had figured he would tell his story first and get it over with, so he built momentum from the start. Herschel's past—especially his mother's death and his father's suicide—took Stephen by surprise. The others in the recovery group hadn't heard as much of his past as Stephen had. The stories of the other three men and four ladies were tragic, in their own right, but Herschel's transparency offered them the freedom to share without holding back. Hershel's heart went out to them. With each one, he begged them in his mind not to repeat the way he had handled Susan's and his child's deaths for so many years.

Herschel showed up week after week. The fog that had settled over his life dissipated more with every passing meeting. He and Stephen began to spend time together outside of their group. One morning, they had settled into a corner booth at a practically empty pancake restaurant. Stephen sat first and reached for the syrup bottle. Herschel joined him and spread jam across his pancakes.

"Is that how you always eat them?" the doctor asked.

"Most of the time. When I was a kid in one of my foster homes, my foster mother handed me pancakes, as usual, after her 'real kids,' as she called them, had used the last of the syrup. I knew better than to complain, so I thought jelly might make them edible. I've been partial to jam ever since, although I suspect I'm still celebrating my childhood ingenuity."

"What's with the six o'clock breakfast? I haven't done many six-in-the-mornings since I moved from the emergency room to private practice. You must have packed your schedule today."

"Actually," Perdue said, glancing around to make sure they were out of earshot, "I wanted to ask you something in private that I'm a little hesitant to bring up in our group."

Stephen put his fork on the table to give his friend his full attention. "Sounds serious."

"It is."

"You can trust me."

"I believe you. Did you... I mean... did you ever, you know... think about, uh, taking your own life?"

The doctor didn't flinch. "Yes, I did. I never bring it up in the group because I don't want to introduce ideas to vulnerable people. But that's part of my story. I'm ashamed to say it because it would have left my kids to go back to a mother who didn't want them. But I was so distraught... Herschel, I need to trust that this stays just between us, at least for now, okay?"

"I promise." Herschel crossed his heart, which drew the slightest of smiles from his friend.

"I didn't just think about it."

"You tried?"

"Sort of. I had been in Birmingham for less than a month, and I had just finished a sixteen-hour shift at the hospital. It was late at night, and I was worn out. I was heading back to my mom's old house—the kids and I stayed there for a while after Mom died until I restored it enough to sell. Her house was out on Garfield Road, and there's a flat straight stretch for about a mile or more."

"I know the spot. We built a treehouse close by some years back."

"Well, like I said, I was dog tired, the weary a good day's sleep wouldn't cure. I didn't think anything about it at first, but I pressed the accelerator, perhaps more than usual. As the car sped up, I kept giving it more and more gas. If you know the stretch, you remember there's a sharp curve at the end of it and a bridge a short distance around the corner. When I reached the halfway point of that stretch of road, I glanced down and realized I was going a ninety miles per hour and still speeding up. Something in me gave up and convinced my exhausted mind it would be better this way, that I would achieve the peace that had been eluding me."

"Did you...?"

"No."

"What kept you from it?"

Stephen laughed at the memory. "Two-thirds of the way down the straightaway, a narrow lane shoots off to the right, but a grove of mature pine trees hides the entrance to it. That's where a cop was sitting. He turned his lights on before I ever got to him. I stopped, knowing I was about to go to jail. If helplessness had jumped in the car with me when I left the hospital, it didn't relent when those blue lights flashed. I pulled over and lowered my window. When that policeman walked up to the car, he found a basket case. I was bawling my eyes out. He asked if I had been drinking and told me to step out of my car.

"When I did, he saw my scrubs and my name tag. I guess he figured I had lost a patient or something, so he asked me what was wrong, not like a cop, but as someone who understood losing a life while on duty to save them. I told him everything and that he could feel good about his shift because he had saved a life that night—mine. Herschel, there's no doubt in my mind the Lord positioned that officer to patrol that specific road on that night to preserve my life."

"Did you go to jail?"

"Didn't even get a ticket."

"What?"

"He said he had just spent a week giving people tickets for going two over the speed limit in front of the major's house, something he had to do about once a year. After everything else I had been through, he didn't have the heart to take me to jail or even give me a ticket, especially after I told him what a model driver I would be from then on. He even gave me a police escort home... with his flashing lights off."

"Wow, Stephen, I didn't realize your hurt ever ran that deep."

"I'm not afraid to tell the story, but I must think about my kids. I'm not sure it would benefit them to realize what I would have done to them that night. It was like a hopeless mood settled over me like a fog rolling across the bay all of a sudden, though, and I was helpless to control it until I saw those blue lights."

"It just came over you, huh?"

"Yes, but the officer insisted I find somebody to discuss my feelings with so *sudden depression*, as he called it, would never come over me again. I told him I would."

"Did you?"

Stephen chewed the rest of his bite of sausage and then took took a bite of his pancakes before he answered. "That's when I first called you, Perdue."

Herschel hung his head. "I'm sorry," he mustered.

"It's okay. I understand your battles enough now to realize you couldn't have helped me because you were still battling your own sorrow."

"I should have dealt with it already. Oh, my goodness, how many other people could I have helped if I had only dealt with my grief?"

"Looking back won't help. Don't do it. Trust me, you can't change anything. Now, you wanted to tell me something outside the group. Perdue, have you been... having thoughts?"

"No, not lately. But I did before we talked at church, at first at random and then more often and with increasing specificity. The day I saw you in church, I had almost reached the breaking point. But there you were, standing with your kids, worshiping like life always worked out for you. I knew different, though, and in that moment, I saw hope for myself, a hope I wish I had offered you."

Stephen clasped his hands in front of himself, looked heavenward, and breathed, "Thank You."

"Anyway, we're getting pretty close to the end of this grief group, and it has done me a world of good. Understand that I haven't been this transparent with anybody since Susan died, but if my recovery was going to be complete, I needed to tell somebody about my thoughts of... you know... suicide."

"I'm glad you did, and thanks for trusting me with that. I recognize it was a big deal for you to come to the group in the first place, but I'm glad the Lord keeps choosing to redeem my worst moment to keep others from theirs."

Struck by inspiration, Perdue asked, "Hey, Doc, you doing anything today?"

"No plans. I cut back to three days a week earlier

this year, and today's an off day. You have something in mind?"

"Nothing on my schedule can't wait until tomorrow. Want to visit some treehouses today?"

"I would love it."

"DAVID, I enjoyed more clarity after the ten weeks in that grief support group than I had since Susan's death. What I didn't realize until later was that Stephen was friends with the fellow on Garfield Road who had the treehouse we had built for him. He had already arranged for our graduation retreat from recovery group to take place in his treehouse. It was beyond cool to spend that time with my group in something I had built, especially since we built it during my early years, back when I was still doing some of the actual labor. We had repaired some squirrel damage one time, but it was still as sturdy as ever."

"That is so cool. I'm glad you could enjoy that. I'll bet when you told Mr. Bradford your vision all those years before, you never saw yourself in that position."

"You're so right. It occurred to me after we finished our grief group that I was still holding onto a little bitterness against God. He never allowed me to build a treehouse for my son since in my mind, God had taken him away from me, even though I can't tell you our child would have been a son. After Susan died, we kept the non-profit going, but my heart wasn't in it for all those years, and nobody else put the passion into it that she did. The number of houses we built for boys' homes was minimal compared to our potential.

"One of the first things I did after I became 'well' again was to see what we could do to return our New Heights program to the level Susan had it. One of the first things I did was to convince a part-time doctor to give up his practice and run it for me. He is doing a phenomenal job getting our houses built at boys homes and ranches all over the country."

"Is doing?"

"Oh, yeah, he hit the ground running, and he's never broken stride. Two of his girls work with him now, and their job is to go on adventures together. We have had Mitchell-Reeves turned in a positive direction for an several years now, and I couldn't be more fulfilled. Our satisfied customers and our old-fashioned paper catalogs are the only advertising we need."

David grinned at the older man's spunk. "You sound like you're still running it." When Perdue's grin stretched across his face, David stopped. "Wait, so you're still... but what about..."

Perdue rose and pushed the door closed. "Leave of absence, David. All the folks here know I'm different from the rest of the old folks at Winding Acres, but they can't figure out why. I tell them I'm writing my life story, and I couldn't have come up with a better cover."

"You mean you're not...?"

"No, I am writing my autobiography. They just don't believe it. The truth makes the perfect cover, don't you think? What would shock them is that I'm not retired. Stephen convinced me to get away and write my story, says I owe it to the world. He gave me the freedom to share his story after he told his girls how close he had come to throwing his life away, and my story is incomplete without his. I never would have written it at all if I had continued to go into the office, so you might say I checked myself in here for a year to write it. I figured, what better place to go than back to the place Mitchell-Reeves Adventures began here in Harriston."

As the clock crept toward three o'clock in the afternoon, almost five hours after Perdue spoke his first words to his amateur window repairman, David asked, "How close are you to finishing your book?"

"Well, my goal was to write it, revise it, and learn it to where I could tell my complete story whenever the Lord gives me the opportunity."

"So, are you close to reaching your goal?"

"You tell me, David Gull."

LONESOME, PARTY OF SIX SERIES

Lonesome, Party of Six

Lonesome Reunion

Two of a Kind: Working on an Empty House

Twenty Years Gone: Lonesome in the Heart of Texas

Broken Pane

Everybody Else's Wedding

www.ingramcontent.com/pod-product-compliance
Lightning Source LLC
Chambersburg PA
CBHW030115260626
47156CB00008B/2674